THE BODY
IN FOUR
PARTS • • •

1 9 9 3

OTHER BOOKS BY

JANET KAUFFMAN

Places in the World a Woman Could Walk

Collaborators

Obscene Gestures for Women

The Weather Book

Where the World Is

THE BODY IN FOUR PARTS · BY JANET KAUFFMAN

GRAYWOLF PRESS

Publication of this volume is made possible in part by a grant provided by the
Minnesota State Arts Board through an appropriation by the Minnesota State
Legislature, and by a grant from the National Endowment for the Arts. Additional
support has been provided by the Jerome Foundation, the Northwest Area
Foundation, the Mellon Foundation, the Lila Wallace – Reader's Digest Fund, and
other generous contributions from foundations, corporations, and individuals.
Graywolf Press is a member agency of United Arts, Saint Paul. To these
organizations and individuals who make our work possible, we offer heartfelt
thanks.

Published by Graywolf Press, 2402 University Avenue, Saint Paul, Minnesota 55114.
All rights reserved. Printed in the United States of America.

2 4 6 8 9 7 5 3
First Printing, 1993

Library of Congress Cataloging-in-Publication Data
Kauffman, Janet.
The body in four parts / Janet Kauffman.
p.   cm.
ISBN 1-55597-179-2 (cloth) :
I. Title. II. Title: Body in 4 parts.
PS3561.A82B6 1993
813'.54—dc20   92-34193

FOR D.M.

IN HER ENTIRETY

CONTENTS

WATER

■ T H E B O D Y

LET'S SAY I have visited my sister, underwater. It's true she has her own place, and it isn't any above-ground capsule – walls, windows, paper, floors. She's in the channel. She's sunk.

It's not a question of coming back, and hanging up a T-shirt to dry. My sister blinks her eyes and turns, a fluid thing. She's with the dangled larvae, nymphs of water bugs, the ones who transform later and breathe – dragonflies, phantom crane flies, whirligig beetles, ephemera, dixa midges. She's one of them. But instead of complicating herself, as they will, and maneuvering to the surface and taking off, water a far-flung memory if it's that, my sister Dorothea stays put, swirls. She's shed her future, in a way, and gone under. She's linked herself to her origins, or you could say exploded herself, beyond everything, the way cataclysmic heat spits molecules off the body. Zsst – water. Zsst – silica, hydrogen.

Dorothea floats. She cavorts. She doesn't have a garden. She doesn't eat out.

On land, my sister kept an arsenal, she was known for it. Half of all she possessed was illegal, and I could hear in her voice, she half-believed it was true when she said, "My left arm, hell, it was smuggled in."

Left arm, right arm, she could make me smile. I know her mind. She had no qualms about violence as a means. She dreamed her own self so often with silken impenetrable skin, with electric hair, tinged blue, metallic, that it came as no surprise to her when she looked down the barrel of a gun, she thought the words, *Lovely hair*.

She tried to fit into nature's scheme, but, out of water, she never figured how to do it without a recoilless weapon.

DOROTHEA. Dorothy. Dot. Dottie.

Dot Dot Dot – she calls herself S. For what, Dottie? Sabotage? Subterfuge?

What would you guess her last name is? That's the murky part. She claims the surname Campbell. A lunch-type name, a blond name. A Pop-Tart breakfast and lunch-box soup name. What about that boiled eels Scottish ballad? No, that's Randal. Lord Randal. This is Campbell. S. Campbell.

She *should* have the same last name as me, isn't that how naming works? Under the usual circumstances. On the usual plank floors.

But S. never owned up to family history. She had this swamp heritage, I suppose. She was a metamorphoser, in and out of the pond water.

S. MAKES NOISES. She takes note. S. registers global shifts of weather, everything down there does, and she registers, too, the microscopic, truly microscopic, twists of cellular material. She misses, I would say, the broad middle of human society, you see how it is. She lives like a single cell, on the one hand; and, on the other, like a giant two-legged woman, straddling our minor constructions, which she probably sees, from that point of view, through the eye of her sex.

She's invisible, submerged; and overarching, monumental. I am glad she no longer speaks. The noises she makes, well, they are incoherent, secret as vaginal sounds, or raucous, mimicking sometimes choral toads, sometimes the shrill underwater *rheeeeee* of mergansers.

"SHE'S A GONER, Babe," my friend Margaretta says.

Margaretta, at the fish stand, places her pearl-rimmed glasses on the countertop. She points a large hand towards the channel. "You have my condolences," she says. "It's too aromatic a season to go and rot."

Margaretta holds a cleaver in her left hand, and she tells me this is the bluest batch of sunfish yet. She sets them out like paintings, six or seven. She arranges them like swimmers.

Margaretta is a friend to me, talking, talking when there is something else to do, or not, she has her nothing-to-lose command of gossip. Her voice is smooth, shaded, dark at the edges. She's stood at the fish stand, at the edge of the channel, all the years I know – sorted, filleted, bought, sold. She smells like the place. There's a sheen, often, to her skin.

Margaretta touches the wide barrette in her hair, mother-of-pearl from a shell, and she sets her elbows on the fish stand. There are blisters on her elbows, she confers that many hours. And days. She confers with anybody – anybody talking, anybody bringing pages for her to read on the subject of water, that in particular, or death by water, or kisses – she reads all this. She says she does not mind murk and mire.

I give her Dorothea's papers. They are damp, hard to read. Even now, somehow, Dorothea writes like crazy.

Margaretta reads a page, she turns on her little fan, up at eye level on the post.

IN FOUR PARTS

The Whale and His Swimmers
— by S. Campbell

The geography of God's lips takes
some telling. To start, his lips are
cradled, couched, one slipper next to
another slipper, two footprints, the
same foot, darkness between.

And speaking, he stammers, stalls.
"Yes, yes, here's a bunch," he says,
"come here."

And his swimmers, oh so be-
draggled, go fishtailing out of
range, they gulp air and dive.

Jonasine surfaces, treads water.

Now God moves his lips, he
smiles at his designs. On shore,
he's watched one brick go up
beside another, he has moved
his whole mouth to laugh at
the flick of a switch.

But out here, without sea legs,
he falters. He swears at nature—
who else — he is restless, he can't

sit down. There's no chair, no shelter sufficient.

"Hey, big-mouth," Jonasine says. That turns him around. He knows his own fabrications, he haunts them. He murmurs, water filling his mouth, "My darlings, now swim to my lips, come inside."

MARGARETTA sets down the papers. She lights charcoal on a grill, a grate on the fish stand, with a stack of kitchen matches. "I'll miss her."

"She's right there," I say. "Right in the channel."

I like the way Margaretta accepts the facts. She doesn't dispute. She likes contradictions, same as me. Dorothea's in the water, there she is. She is water. Dorothea's my sister. And so close sometimes, we match. She's the damp on my skin. The wet in all the cells. I tell Margaretta about my brother Jean-Paul, the one on fire. Jack, in air.

"We're all in this together. It's much worse for the brain to deny these things," I say.

Margaretta doesn't argue. She doesn't smirk. She says, "Babe, we are complex creatures, I know that much."

Margaretta grills her sunfish crisp. She likes the char on her teeth. Blue smoke takes some narrow turns upward, hangs around like blue hair, and then it's gone in the scented wind up the channel.

Bricks in the neighborhood, saturated with fish smoke, press peculiar ideas into the heads of lovers who lean against the walls. They buy

Margaretta's fish, of course, but they also recline, longer than anybody really believes, discussing underwater life, among the mosquitoes of the channel, in the mud, too, their white shorts mucked with clay, mud on their knees and elbows. These are people in trouble when they get home, and Margaretta's part of the city has gained a reputation for clumsiness, on account of excuses these lovers fabricate. The area is more imaginative than most lowland communities. And more knowledgeable on the subject of chimney crayfish, for instance. Daily lovemaking has improved, too, which may, all along, have been Margaretta's wish.

MY SISTER Dorothea, in the house at one time, showed off her weapons. On the table, she lined up her knives in their blue velvet cases. She hauled out the rifles, revolvers. She said guns were as good as money in the bank.

Dorothea purchased handguns, every caliber, replica blackpowder pistols with steel case-hardened frames, hammers, and loading levers, belt knives, magnum folding lockback knives, ammo kits, deburring tools, shotguns, you name it. She locked them away.

What did she think could happen?

All right, anything could happen.

A body might as well, she said, be armed to the teeth.

She picked a gun from the table, she polished it with a cotton rag. It shone very blue, burnished. She sorted out ammunition, and methodically, she loaded the gun, she unloaded it.

At the table, she sat like a suicide, gun in hand, barrel aimed at her eyeball.

With the pull of the trigger, she squinted and watched the interior mechanisms click. The steel bore reflected small lights, ricocheted them around in the barrel like headlights in water, like highlights, she said, in healthy hair.

OVERLAPPING should be the name of the place. We've got it all: simultaneous weathers, the ancient elements – air, earth, fire, water – embodied, disembodied. Intersections of purple loosestrife, bottles and cans, concrete walkways, semiautomatic weaponry, duckweed.

Oh, you can say that a city is separate from everything else, but, listen, you can say anything. The city's right in the middle of wilderness, look around, air in the same configurations, and don't tell me swampland isn't jammed up, like a downtown district, bottlenecked, replete with ruin.

Ignore the simpleminded Jean-Paul, my brother, saying one is one, and another is definitely another. He and S. have their problems, but in this, they agree – the cataloguing mind, trim, erect, yes sir and no sir, city and country, fish and fowl. They are the military ones, shoes in pairs, be a good sport. S. is overly impressed with the cut of Jean-Paul's coat, his pouty lower lip that tastes of river water the way he says Paris tastes.

When we argue, S. and Jean-Paul on one side, their own battalion, that is a rout, but prolonged, with hair pulling, and once in a mirror, I saw my own hands close on a mess of strands.

"EH BIEN, dis donc," Jean-Paul says, dismissive. Or, more often, "Bah! Dis donc." He pulls on his black shirt and butt-snug Pont Neuf pants and drives out near River Rouge to the Green Door, where he claims the front booth by the six-foot amp. He sits sideways, his back against the wall, feet on the vinyl bench, embery hair in a ponytail with its silk tie. You might as well knot up fire with black cotton string. He knows how.

Somebody asks him to dance and he's out there, and then you see how talk is a sit-down version of hind-legged dance. A sit-up version of laid-down love. Jean-Paul takes it good and easy.

This is one place we all go, all of us together, without one lording it over another and churning the stomach sour.

The drummer in the band doesn't blink, he sees it all. He looks me in the eye and sees it all – dancing water women, firebrands, buzzards, boulders, fish.

We look pretty good when the music starts.

THEY RATTED and rearranged my hair, this was long ago, and that was the first I noticed a multiplicity, touches flat-fingered, a baptizing preacher's touch. Desirous. Another blessed hand. Hair one way, then fingers like combs taking it the other way, and chill air on the scalp, where there'd been no chill. They accompanied me. An accumulation, an adhesion. Proliferations. Mind overlapping mind – the dampness of my sister; something more like weathers, twinned, with brothers.

You're not so sure about the brothers? My brother Jack, the three a.m. breeze?

You laugh.

Well, I laughed, too. Jack, brother air, brother bone-dry and sere. Santa Ana. Sirocco.

Brother Jean-Paul with fire on his head.

THESE ARE NOT, in the end, subdivisions. You can't subtract from a climate. They appear. They thrive. Dorothea underwater. Jean-Paul in flames. Jack in air.

It takes a long time, you can imagine how long it takes, to claim these claimants. They comb your hair. And mine is a human body, an earth and clay-shaped body, just the usual blockwork and mortar and fancy pottery!

I turn to mud when I am Dorothea.

THIS IS NOT a classic case. Nobody's got a file with interviews. If you want the documentation of a disorder, multiple personality disorder, say, if that's what you want to know, you'll have to read the other accounts. Nobody's driven their navy blue cars out to study this.

But it may be, in its essentials, a commonplace phenomenon: a body in numerous parts – Dorothea, Jean-Paul, Jack, and me – male, female, brother, sister, water, fire, air, you name it, walking around on the ground, all-in-one.

I wouldn't call it a problem, but a resolution. Consider the possibilities. If a child can assemble sixteen or sixty selves, to survive the horrors attendant upon abuse, then I suppose four brothers and sisters are not too many, to survive – what would you call it? – *elemental* deprivation? Drastic loss of touch. The way we put on hats and keep away air. The way the elements hide in the cells and we walk around, unaware. Even of oxygen, for instance. Blue air. Leaves and their component carbons, as everyday things. Sister and blood-brother leaves. Mud. Rock. The family before any other.

IN   FOUR   PARTS

Why say we are human only? I can't say it. The heart of me, you know it, is rock. I don't call this metaphor, no. The rock doesn't have a name, it doesn't move. But there could come a time. What I mean is: deprived of the elemental world – and who isn't, with a globe divided, the whole planet sectioned, roofed, cut and pasted – even its waters – what can a body do, if it is a body, but acknowledge, salvage, the elements in its own boundaries. Draw them out. Wring them out. Host. House. It's nothing out of the ordinary – you've probably got a snow or drought brother under your skin, too. Why not let the boy speak? A part of the body, anyone's body, longs for a green, a blue, mud-enmired planet, with its own turnings and feedings and comings and goings. Something apart from the human. That's all. That's not much to ask. But it doesn't sell, does it? It can't be sold. So, deprived of clay and sand-sweet ground, and air, water wherever it falls, fire – which is how many other elements in one? – and you can guess all of the other essentials, I've only named four, the most plain-faced, look at it this way, it's possible that the body has summoned its lost geographies. Or retrieved what the body alone comprehends. Well, you read Ovid, say – there's Daphne in leaves. The simple sea-changes. Cadmus and wife, embraced, entwined, serpentine. There you have it. But this is the modern world – the metamorphoses go in any direction: water, machinery, cloud, objects strange or ordinary. A plumber's snake. When necessary.

No, this is no psychological malady. If it's a malady at all. I'm gainfully employed. I'm no hazard to myself, or to others. Is Dorothea? No, no hazard in the water. No hazard now that she's under the water, turned to it – where she's at home.

In the usual cases, you read about integration of all those selves, as an appropriate thing. But in a renegade case, I don't know. What can we do? – we are already closely related. We are not strangers to one another. We cohabit a habitat. I'd say it makes sense. At least it makes sense of the senses. Don't tell me it's only metaphorical. Or at least, if you say that, mention the metaphorical climates, as well – temperate, tropical, sub-tropical, on one planet. There are climates within climates, too – in the vicinity of volcanoes, in high-rise corridors, at the edges of lakes, under the chin, behind the knees.

WHAT A REVERSAL, our mothers and fathers orphaned, orphaned of children, sons and daughters gone to the elements, and all the parental couplets, orphaned in the sandstone institutions. Psychology wrenched in reverse, it's been overturned, you could say, or you could say geology has caught up. In the first days, it was like reading backwards, but of course time continues rolling and the elements accumulate and then deteriorate, it is a planet of collections and dissolutions. Well, it is like the smell in the air before rain – the Guernsey cow smell over the gravel road, the outspreading diesel fumes, the faintest purpling. Sisters and brothers turn out digressive, deteriorative – you'd think we would all be used up, and used to it by now, paper crumbling to grit and the billboards peeling down easily after the rain. S. used to say this progress follows the sensible pattern of mowing lawns every week, the grass thick from torrential rains, the cut grass in long windrows, aquamarine then rat brown, and the scent luxurious at first, it is flower and leaf, and then it is the sickly smell of rat and fur and whatever you smell in the northwest corners of rooms, pungent, low to the floor. It could be the smell of sex, yes, it could be. The smell of the body's ointments, the crush of cells into one another, sweat, and the declarations of decay.

I N F O U R P A R T S

MARGARETTA fillets her fish, one cut, two cuts. Three. "Dorothea didn't use a gun?"

I hand her more pages. "No, she didn't."

"That's good. That's good. So she's in one piece."

"She seems fine."

> The Pearl in the Oyster
> — by S. Campbell
>
> Jonasine was the pearl in the oyster. She'd begun as sand, or something turned toward uselessness, like a comma., That's about how she looked at the start. Isolate, nameless. Until the processes of time in the sea, slower than here, but continuous, lay down deposits, adhesions of mineral, like coats and hats on her, fashion upon fashion. She grew large, iridescent. Her voice changed. It was throatier, with a rasp and richness to it, attractive to men.
>
> "Honey, Pearl," her Daddy said. "How about a song?" He set her

up on a cushion and stepped back. "Go right ahead."

It was a crowd — hoteliers, tourists, birders, realtors, one or two pop stars, farmers, network and cable TV crews on furlough, and at the piano, always a fair accompanist, the Gravedigger in his tux.

Jonasine cued him, "One-two-three, one-two-three." And she sang:

> Here in the wa-ter-y
> Home of the fishes I
> Long for a politic,
> Sin-u-ous, sens-u-ous
>
> Man. Is he here now? Where?
> Man is he here now where

Jonasine slurred the words of the Man refrain — a plaintive question at first, but tongued a few times, a diminishment set in, a breakage of individual words to nothing

much more than themselves.
Romance lost out in this treatment,
as you'd expect.

Jonasine's voice was serene, then
surly, then dismissive.

If the Gravedigger had paid
some attention, and tossed her
his top hat, she could have
easily twirled it, slung it behind her, kicked it with her
spike heel, and caught it again
with the flamboyance, the
particular arrogance, of any woman
hired to entertain men. There could
have been, for the audience, that
satisfaction — the grand finale.
As it was, her Daddy clapped his
hands, frowning, and the ones in
the crowd with some knowledge
of sea environments applauded, too.
They could see the phenomenal
stretch of Jonasine's talent. A few
tourists were already composing
phrases for postcards. The words

grotesquerie and *velveteen* figured in almost every account. A realtor, who wanted to say *unbelievable*, decided against it, and wrote: "In the belly of the whale, you see everything but the bullets flying."

THERE IS a part of me that is old, and it is of course the heart. The rest of me, no, it is flimsy with youth. And, looking around, I can see this deformity in a large part of the country's population – among numbers of people who try to do nothing. Nothing to make a profit, or news.

I'm not alone – we are the ones who do everything else.

I'LL TELL YOU one of the numerous things I do. I take a sack, washable in the channel, and along the edges of roads, in chicory stalks, quack grass, and Queen Anne's lace, I find cans. Many people do.

"You could do so much more," Jean-Paul says.

And *there* is an argument that dead-ends.

Sometimes I discover brown long-necked bottles made of glass. I am thinking long-legged bottles, but there are no such things, are there!

I collect the cans in alleyways and in the gutters, out of the wastebaskets in large buildings. It is a fair-weather job, collecting these materials and dropping them in the muslin sack. Pick and trade, a simple song. Jean-Paul cannot be convinced. Even when the sack is full, and it fills up daily, this is not a heavy load to carry. My delivery point – the Super One store with the highly successful crushing machine – lies three blocks from all other points.

In the foyer of the store, the collection woman behind the barrier talks to her friend in the first aisle, and she never says to me "You again" when I haul up the sack. She takes it. She has long fingers with purple polish on the nails, and these beautified fingers lift each can from the sack and, according to brand or color, she places them in a tunneled chute leading to a bin. When she has finished sorting, she pushes an orange button and the machine crushes the cans with a mild collapsing sound, undramatic, and when it quiets, she hands me the dollar bills, with her purple nails pointing up at her chin as she counts them out.

Endorado, I believe her name is.

But in fact she wears a tag on her white smock, and her name is Shelley. I wonder about her life in another place, without her friend to talk to, and without the turns back-and-forth between sack and machinery.

Shelley talks to her friend about lottery numbers and about someone named Mike who has purchased two rifles and a compound bow.

Endorado is quiet. Endorado knows nothing about those things.

I CAN SAY THIS about myself, and it could be said across the board: she is piecemeal, she is not herself, she's numberless, not numb, she cannot be counted out, she's gusted air, open fire, she is not watered down, she's dirt and debris. Also, she is a hank of hair, hacked.

MY HAIR has never been cut by a hair professional.

A rarity, but even so, not something unknown. There are other heads and hairs uncared for by the trained hands and catalogued *materiel* of the beauticians. Still, an oddity, yes, when there are kitchen beauty shops on your street as well as mine and then, too, the carpeted and chrome-hooded salons wherever a person shops. The fervor and the aroma of hairdressing establishments seduce. That is what they do. They intend seduction. They pull you in, an insider. It's secret, very sweet and perfumed, like the rooms of the mortician. Oh I don't mind the pungency and seating arrangements, the layout of taxidermy, but what about the monopolies on purities — bowls, baths, dyes, the specialized use of cotton swabs and curling devices, electric drying machines. But I do walk by, and I look in there at the machinery and the pastels, and I breathe what I can of the permanent-wave air waves.

Margaretta goes to the hairdresser, once a week. "Religiously," she tells me. She says, "Yes, I am off to the sanctuary." Or, "I am off to the laboratory." And she does come back with her shoulders, as well as her hair, transporting the fragrances of floral rinse, incense, sponged-on ammonia, aromas of the devout. Her hair some days returns so smooth and shined it falls like satin cloth. It sways with a *shush* when she reaches down in the buckets behind the counter to pull out fish. She slaps the fish on the waxy paper and turns to the side for the cleaver, *shush*. "A golden cap," she says. Or else her hair is pitch black. Or else it is tinted towards blue, a dark gray going on dark blue, and then the hairdo swoops up, defies the gravity of Margaretta's wrists, up and back in a stern wave so that, were Margaretta not wearing fishbone earrings spray-painted chartreuse, she would stand there, agèd fishwife, the hair colors and angles suggesting, in the abstract, decrepitude.

I HAVE NOT allowed the scissors of the hair professional to redesign my hair. But, as with Samson, somebody got at it.

On the front porch, headed in, at that last step before the hand reaches for the door handle, Dorothea gestures and makes her sounds, "What did you do to your hair, Babe?" She is dripping wet, out on the porch, and she points to me, to the storm window, the top-to-bottom reflection of myself.

I am wearing my round-toed black rubber pig boots, which I wear for morning walks to the channel and into the channel if that's what I feel like. To notice the sluggish current and the assortments of snails, a person has to step in the water, stand there a long while, and not flinch when mosquitoes land on the broad strip of forehead between the eyebrows, a place they love, a delicate cushioned stretch of skin, very slight padding over bone, well it must be delectable – that is where mosquitoes present themselves and sting. I let them. I suit their purposes, and they don't interfere with mine.

I wear heavy pants, a long-sleeved shirt, although I roll up the sleeves in the sunlight. No hat. I would not wear a hat. Hair is a hat, I tell this to Dorothea, and my hair ordinarily shunts back at the sides, a stringy brown in winter and in summer, more or less yellowed. The hair stiffens in summer and coils, haphazard, even if I comb it, and I do comb it in the mornings as a way of limbering up, the way I yawn, throw back my elbows.

Still, the storm window contains a surprise and I acknowledge it: my hair is swooped off to the side and tied up, askew, with a green twist tie from a trash bag.

Loose strands of hair jut on both sides. A considerable chunk of hair has been scissored away, that's how it looks. No, it appears to be chopped, knife-cut.

S. suggests it could be the work of Jack.

But then she is back to her business in the channel, and I think it through for myself: it is Dorothea who has the weapons.

I write her a legible note:

> S., This appears to be the work of your Buck Special knife. Is it?
>
> Would I? Your friend, S. Campbell.
>
> Why would you deny it?
>
> Have I denied it? Signed, S.

The questions are plain, you see the hooked marks, we have that between us, and yes, you see the reluctance to answer *anything*.

UNDER THE ROCK at the channel, S. keeps her papers. She writes with indelible ink, but even so, the decay is continuous, irreversible. When she shows me a page, the patterns of mud streaks, more distinct than handwriting, almost make more sense.

But Dorothea points to the words, and she gives the papers to me.

I look at the pages. They don't look like paper. They're iridescent, with the moisture, the press of the rock press, the blurring of ink chemicals into the page. The paper looks like shell, or the dark skin of the winkle snail, *Viviparus intertextus*.

In the Belly of the Whale
— by S. Campbell

Jonasine saw the belly of the whale the way Bible illustrators saw it: a cathedral room with ribs arched overhead for the dome. It was a Disney digestive tract, in and out through the room.

Jonasine stood on the backbone — did the whale swim belly up? — to keep her footing when the water and fishes washed through.

There was no telling how she got there. But she knew the place backwards and forwards. She felt at home. In her spare time she stood on stepladderlike heaps of bone trash and charted with her hands the silky membranes of the whale's interior. She knew the pores and dimples of the whale's gut as well as she knew the creases and rigid scars on her own arms.

She wasn't alone. Jonah was there. Alfred. A few others. They fished with their makeshift thread lines, hooks of hatpins. They did all right.

Even so. "It's too much the life of the mind," Jonasine said. "There's too much guesswork."

Seeing her life as a kind of abstraction, she turned her attention to the environs. She mapped the whale tissues especially in the most difficult areas, where tendon joined bone, the cells of attachment. She studied the life cycles of the parasites on the whale's digestive cilia. She observed herself as parasite, too. She didn't miss that. She began to speculate about other possible whale life, other possible hosts.

A detail from her daily life to make note of here is this particular scene: Jonasine making love with Alfred. Jonasine too often observed herself, not so much in the act, but in the preliminaries — the habitual enticements, exchanges of food, close conversation. It was clear to her these were customs of approach. She did not magnify events into personal drama. She was in the belly of a whale. She would not let herself exaggerate.

Instead, Jonasine found her pleasure in diminishment. It made more sense. There was no aim, no gung-ho call of progress, not here.

In lovemaking, Jonasine said to herself, "I am a body," or "This is a body," or better yet, "Oh, we are bodies only," and her skin softened and her legs pushed like water against Alfred. She felt the bend in her elbows. She felt a warmth between her eyebrows and her eyelids.

she did not think, He is a good man. She did not think, We will live in the West. She did not think _love_, either as noun or verb, or if she did, her mind cooled her off as completely as if she'd reached over and opened a heavy text.

And so when they leaned into the pillowed walls of the whale, Jonasine said to herself, We are bodies only. When Alfred touched his tongue to her ear, she heard the words, Bodies only. She felt the give of her cells, muscle and bone, when they held each other and coiled their legs together or coiled their entire bodies together, legs pulled up strangely behind the other's back.

Their two bodies, indeterminate cells, brought to each other their variable shapes, their heat, their hair, the several orifices of ex-

change, their benign underwater sounds.

They were bodies within a body. And the more simply they saw themselves, the more complexly they were linked to the whale, who swam them through oceans they could not remember or dream.

DOROTHEA, naked except for her black tennis shoes and her black-rimmed glasses, walked across the gravel at the fish stand. She kept on going, down the walkway onto the packed-mud path, pushed aside, out of habit, the bur-reed and loosestrife. She was wearing absolutely nothing. And you know she could not have been wholly comfortable, even in the dark, even in the dark she was apparent as a large fish, or marmot, walking on awkward hind legs. But, no, she was graceful enough, that's how she was. She often walked to the channel, her thighs didn't recoil from the roughness of the saw-toothed grasses. She walked the way she always walked. The skin on parts of her body, though, hadn't toughened from ordinary exposure, and maybe for that reason the mosquitoes hesitated a second or two before stinging, and her forward-goingness kept them trailing her, she was shadowed by mosquitoes. Moths took to her, like a light, and she didn't mind, she felt their furred bodies and simplicity of intent. The air registered cold, air off ice, on her belly and on her breasts, places foreign to moving air. In daylight, clothed, Dorothea was a woman whose arms were definitive – her arms made her way, her elbows worked like antennae, her hands were her whole body's hands. But now – she was belly-woman. She felt the world reoriented – she might as well have been walking backwards, everything approached and receded against expectation. Oncoming air hit her below the navel and washed up around her breasts and around her face. Her arms didn't make much difference. She didn't have to feel her way, darkness was not very dark because that was the whole of it, and even the night-boats out past the channel markers took the last turn away, like a turn downhill, and night-lights were out in the warehouses.

Near the edge of the water, Dorothea pushed at a flat rock with her foot, then tipped it up. Underneath the rock from her cache of paper, she took one piece and like a store clerk preparing a purchase, she folded her glasses, she wrapped them up. She set the package on the ground.

She took off her tennis shoes. In one step, she reached the water.

She walked in. Several more steps.

The water rose to her knees even though the channel was not knee-deep at that path-end, but her feet sank into the silt and thick clouds of mud rose between her toes and broke on the surface, vague puffs, disrupting glints off the Gravedigger's shovel, the one reflective surface in the vicinity.

The Gravedigger said, "Dig."

They do that sort of thing, give the order, chase the green darners off the surface, and there you are.

I'd ask a few questions first, but S. is obliging. She took her time, she folded her glasses, that's how she did it. She folded them up and wrapped them in typing paper. Here they are. She untied her shoes and set them together.

The Gravedigger handed the shovel to Dorothea. She took it.

How do you measure difficulty in matters without human measure? It may be the hardest part was stepping out of the house. It may be that by this time, in her water-way of living, nothing she did was more strange than opening a door. Digging a grave underwater would, I am sure of it, have taxed the muscles of S.'s shoulders, but the idea of digging would not have caused her distress. With the resumption of usefulness to her arms, S. may have found the shoveling of load after load of bottom mud, that mire, restorative. She did the digging and the Gravedigger did nothing. There are always supervisors, and you have to wonder why. Endorado completes her tasks at Super One and where, you wonder, is her supervisor? Collecting handshakes?

The Gravedigger did his job, standing around, that is all a person can say.

Dorothea dug into the floor of the channel until there was the length and width for her to lie down. She tested the depth from time to time, stepping into the hole until she could walk the space of it, up to her neck. When the dimensions were right, she tossed the shovel to shore.

She pushed her arms out from her sides, then over her head, her fingers pointed for a fine dive.

And over she went, smooth as a dolphin.

She rolled and stretched herself on her back, on the bottom. The mud clouded out around her from the disturbance, but then as she stilled herself, it settled again, a sheet on the body, fine and clay-colored as face powder, even on the nails of her thumbs, which lay in the cups of her hands, at her sides.

S. is supremely at ease in water. She always was.

WHAT DOES the Gravedigger get out of this? Another brick for his house, a garageful of shovels, extra zeroes in his pay? Nobody I know wants to guess. He can say, Dig. But can he say anything else? I guess not.

And since he didn't ask questions, Dorothea didn't answer. She didn't have to account for anything.

I WOULD LIKE to buy Dorothea a gift. But she has denounced possessions and has no ordinary needs. What sort of debris would suit her?

Dorothea, underwater, is not a good citizen. She is no consumer. These years – or any divisions of hours – flow past her in the literal way another person might dream: those blue-cloud dreams when it's wind that moves a day into night, when trees thrash and seasons obliterate themselves very simply.

Dorothea walks in the house, dripping. She takes my hand, she says in her garbled way, "Turn on the TV," but then she finds a mattress on the floor and falls asleep. She's never awake for the closing credits. Adventure shows are her first choice, where cars pile up in ravines, and gunshots, percussive, hit every surface in the room – fabric, steel, wood, water, bone – but the shows aren't violent enough to suit her. She wants nobody spared. She thinks that's the truth they only begin to explore.

"Wishful thinking," is what she mumbles, halfway through. Then she yawns.

When she wakes and asks "Who's left?" and I tell her, she shakes her head. "Nobody makes it," she says.

JEAN-PAUL notices the bad cut of my hair, he's alert to looks. He stands in the door, leans against the doorframe, a casual posture that pinches the shoes on his feet. He never relaxes, not completely. His hair burns on his head. He says, point-blank, "Jack did it, don't blame Dorothea."

I don't blame anybody. It's chopped hair, that's all. I'm as strong as ever.

JACK WOULDN'T do it. Jack is a hand swiping the air, one of those huffs at the corner. He's the one you don't see.

It's a good wind blows nobody ill, an ill wind blows nobody good, whichever it is, a Jack-proverb turned to confuse and make itself strange. I won't take proverb tests. Jack is ill, good, wind, a kite, the buzzard on the silo, wings askew, hello there Jack.

Fraternal twins only, Jean-Paul and Jack bear no resemblance to each other. Jack's invisibility, you can understand, guarantees that. And he is light-handed, a soft improbable voice, he never takes charge, it is why we are lovers, brother or no. He shuts the door of the room. He combs my hair. He says, "If we were together thirty years, I wouldn't regret it, I wouldn't have missed a thing." He kisses me on the feet, his tongue slides between my toes. It is possible in the dark to hold him, although his shape is problematic. I say, "Jack, is that you." And he says "Yes." Or "No." Either way, he moves closer and with a body propertied like air, he surrounds me. What a breeze. We talk about rain, and Dorothea, he has never seen her. I'm glad we don't talk about money. He buys only fine things, and I care nothing about those things. He brings music, the best music, and I say, "Jack, I'd rather listen to you." But then he is silent, completely silent, and I listen to cellos, and then I listen to Roar A-borealis, and then I listen to *Manon Lescaut*, and then I listen to sitars, and then I listen to Muddog Bones.

I HAVE thought of a gift. Watercress.

It's a nothing gift, for anybody but Dorothea.

Floating greens, white-rooted in moving water – S. has made trips upstream every March to find it, and failed. We both recall a particular limestone spring in the East, thick with cress, dark-leaved, bank to bank, obscuring the stream flowing out. That may be the only past a body is able to retrace. A green waterway. One you can eat your way across.

If I located watercress and collected bucketfuls and rerooted it near to Dorothea, even in the channel it would grow for a while before summer slowed the current. In wet years she'd have the green leaves, with that bite on the tongue they give, growing there, practically over her head.

But there's no way to walk to the springhouses you remember, not now, and of course you never could, they are never set right there undisturbed, except in the mind, that is the only pastoral place that's ever been, and you can't just walk there, can you, and scoop out buckets of cress?

Also, it is difficult to walk anywhere in water without Dorothea accompanying, fishlike – she knows the waterways blind, she's memorized the various channels, swamp to creek to river bend. Sometimes out there, she's under my feet, or off to the side, swimming. S. kicks up water with her feet as a signal, or moves with her shadowy butterfly strokes.

The question will be how to shake her, dodge her, catch her out to sea.

She'd call the watercress idea foolhardy, doomed. But doomed is nothing new, not to a landlocked body with cut hair.

I know this. If watercress rooted over her head, S. wouldn't destroy it. She'd lie there and watch it float. She'd grab a fistful. On the sly, she'd chew some stalks, leaves the size of thumbnails. And then, like me, she'd do nothing a few days and watch them grow back.

THE CHANNEL at night smells of the sulfur and belly-must of lightning bugs, if you catch them and smell the palm of your hand. The lightning bugs hang about, closeup and miles off, three-dimensional flickerings of light, cool intermittent lights, they are everywhere across the channel, here and there, untraceable, it is magical, dream-through light, and that is what makes me shut my lips and smile.

I've got Dorothea's Buck Special knife, she left it on the sink, that is her carelessness. No, she is not careless. That is her truth-telling. Her other weapons are locked away and nobody has the key.

I stretch my arm back, my toes dig in the elephant grass where it is dry. The grass rattles.

Dorothea lies in that channel strip of black, low ahead, flat as a cloth streamer, making her frog noises and not noticing me, until I pitch the knife, and it flies, and it tumbles, it cuts the water, and then, you don't have to see this, S.'s pleasures are so well known, she opens her mouth and laughs, too. She makes her move, she catches it, by the blade.

EARTH

■ T H E   B O D Y

■   ■   ■   ■   ■   ■   ■

MARGARETTA has a car, we won't have to walk.

She has her hair done – black silk – she sells her last fish. Margaretta is coherent, American through and through, you could say – she is in-corporated.

She is a fishmonger, good for her. When you look at her, believe me, you can see her. Her breasts hang low, push off to the sides, they are not obscured by vinyl aprons. And when she wears a swimsuit, I have seen this once, she looks amphibious, buoyant, a body adapted for floating across fresh or saltwater seas and then stepping onto land, weighted, ready to walk uphill or roll into bed. I've never asked her age, she could be within any number of decades. I've seen Margaretta drink beer from bottles, both with men and with women, at the Redfish Café, and I've wondered about her sexual life. She seems to be wholly sexual. Is that possible? An all-out sexual human being, in the way you could say a creature – beetle, fox, green-backed heron – is sexual? In her buying and selling of fish, her eating, her drinking, her talk, her reading, her comb-ing her hair, her use of the aquamarine Porta-John by the channel, her sleep, her yawning – she is a body, that's who she is. It is easy to picture her making love. And at length. Any number of ways. This is no easy thing to picture, as you know, when you think of most citizens of the country. Ordinary people, friends, cashiers. But especially the people we are directed to look at – elected officials, male or female, they are so well-suited in cut and layered suits, and film stars, male or female, they are so much photographed, stilled, arranged for seduction. But seduction is not sex. And sex, the sexual act, as an activity, is what a person would think of, looking at Margaretta. She is not provocative, not seductive, but you look at her, you think mouth, and breasts, and belly, vagina, buttocks, you think of the asshole and sphincter, you think of wrists and teeth and earlobes, the hairless palms and the bone blades across her back. You think all of this together, without really thinking, the way you think, when you swallow, of tongue and esophagus, as if your brain were connecting liquid and cartilage, water and channel.

Margaretta is body-in-process. Woman-at-work. Tax-paying American citizen, naked when she is naked. In other words, she is living, in the vicinity. That's a corrollary to her own words, in fact, when she drinks a beer with a fish-affiliated friend, or anybody else, she raises her glass, "Well, we're not dead yet." And her partner at the fish stand, inhaling, registering with some surprise several distinct aromas in the air, clicks glass to glass and affirms, for his or her part, "Man, you said it."

MARGARETTA bought the last Plymouth Horizon off the lot on Fourth Street. She paid cash, worn hand-to-hand bills she'd stacked up selling sunfish.

"It is goddamn sky-blue," she told me, when she offered the car for the trip East, our turnabout drive for the watercress.

Winter had worked its way into and out of the water. I thought my way through it, hibernative, Jack's air blowing across my eyes, he never sleeps. My eyes – this is one way to see it – didn't close for months.

Margaretta hauled a red auger onto the ice of the channel and drilled and fished. She unhooked bluegills, even the smallest ones, onto the ice, and they flipped, curled. They froze in a minute into crescent shapes, like dry leaves. Litter.

I picked them up and pitched them in a bucket. We sat on cushions on the ice, conversing on the subject of cress. Watercress. Not salad cress, the frilled, small-leaved, windowsill variety. But watercress. The pungent in-the-wild rarity (here), commonplace (someplace), you don't need anything on it but salt, to feast. A cure-all, I believe, for Dorothea, done with out-of-water living.

"A cure-all," Margaretta said, "for you, too?"

The trip to collect the plants was in fact an idea Margaretta cooked up, watching the blue hole in the ice: "Go East, *mesdames*, go East. Fuck holy grails," she said, with her homegrown feminist finesse. "You want these greens, okay. This is the opposite of conquest, Babe. No gold-encrusted shit. They ask, Ladies, what do you want? We say, A god-damned decent *salad!*"

I KNOW it sounds small, four buckets of watercress as a gift. But for Dorothea, swimming down there with her fluid arms and rejection of utensils – what could be more suited to her. Dottie and I, as children – when she was already water-inclined – hiked to a springhouse in a field near the Susquehanna, every week in March. S. walked nonstop into the water, as if it were so much low-lying air. She ate as many plants as she picked.

Margaretta has heard my description of the field, the meandering stream farther down, the mud banks, the oxbow cutoffs, the walk-through pipe under Oyster Point Road, and she believes she can track this place down. It's conceivable, with a car. Not too many miles from the Susquehanna. A springhouse, with stone slab steps outside, down to the watercress – if memory means a thing. And if memory doesn't mean a thing anymore – it often doesn't, so much has disappeared – there must be a spring of fresh water, spared, *somewhere*. In some state. Other than the dreaming mind, yes – what are the odds?

It doesn't matter, we've got nothing to lose, looking.

"Springs don't disappear. They don't *all* clog up," Margaretta says. "We only need one."

That's right. We can drive. We have a car. We know what we're look-ing for. A well-defined ecosystem, a small scene. Water charged out of rock. Flowing, stone-cold all year. Dark slate-green leaves, round like shamrock leaves but fleshed, random, sprawled. Edible leaf-green stalks. Edible roots, a few, like fine twine, white and floating. It all floats, and some living things – bird-footed birds, the tiger beetles – walk right across.

MARGARETTA'S sky-blue Horizon looks like vacant space when she drives up. A traveling chunk of air. But she sees it differently. "No, look here, it's a boxcar," she says, shaping it there in the open for me, squaring off the corners.

"Like the boxcars outside of Coatesville. Real boxcars." She is talking about the migrant camp, the start of her teenage life. "Real stinking box-cars. Off of the tracks, hauled in a field. That was a place to drive out of."

Margaretta pats the roof of the Horizon, then opens the hatch, and we load up my carry-on sack, four new galvanized buckets.

"Did you bring any towels? Get towels," Margaretta says.

She's seeing, I know it, she looks ahead, the end-of-travel: where we bend at the spring, arms in the water, we lean farther, and then we walk in, what the hell, ice water up to our knees, armloads of cress.

"I brought tapes," she yells towards the porch. "Some goddamn weepy Caruso."

We check the maps, and Margaretta tells me about the get-out-of-it dream she and her mother had, one or the other of them, every night in Coatesville. One or the other, they sawed circles for windows in the box-car walls, then took the wood circles as wheels, nailed them to the car, and rolled out of camp. Her mother held the maps, Margaretta steered.

"In my mother's dream, of course, *she* drove," Margaretta says. "Otherwise, identical dreams. Into town, down the road, into Philly, over the Delaware. We always headed East. The boxcar could cross water. Any surface."

One day at work, Margaretta's mother found a handsaw in a field, between two cucumber rows. A saw lying out there in the middle of the field. They took it back and hung it up on a nail.

"That could be what did it," Margaretta explains. "A saw on a nail – that's what I see in my head *to this day* when I breathe easy."

THE SUSQUEHANNA below Harrisburg, where the river widens out and opens up for the Chesapeake, was home territory for Margaretta. And it was for me.

In a general way, as children we shared the same backyard – sloped, porous soils, red clay, gray limestone outcrops spouting springs, and water draining everywhere down to the streams, to the Susquehanna. Margaretta and I never met, not there. But we had the lay of the land in common, and play-yards, or boxcar backyards in common, with no standing water.

No wonder we can talk.

Now in the Midwest, we are united by ground and waterways once again. But here it's the glacial dumps of gravel, the only hills we've got, and the pockets of runoff clay, spongy peat, swamp between the dumps. Hills and holes.

Here, something is always waterlogged. Standing in water. Herons, humans, poles for electric wires. Unless the ground is artificially drained – red clay tiling in the past, or bright yellow plastic tiling now, buried, collecting and funneling the water invisibly, underground for miles, to one of the Great Lakes or to one of the visible rivers, the Maumee, the Grand – those few blue lines on maps that end at the blue-tinted Lakes.

My god, dirt and water! What about roads, you say, and names of places, you shake the map, I hear it. What about auto body shops, TV ads and billboards, what about the high-school football team, and Joseph Blue. Whose car is in whose garage? Which sidewalks expanded into which subdivisions in 1975? Name the boys the Green-Eyed Sisters captured during recess. Which Republican president this time, which money scandal? What about Coatesville downtown, how did it get that mining town brick-and-soot look? In which century? What about the color of Margaretta's mother's skin?

You want background, yes, that's what you're looking for.

But background is not a clear-cut issue. "There's no such thing,"

Margaretta says. And here she is surefire, uncompromising. "Dorothea makes sense to me, don't bother explaining."

We turn onto the turnpike ramp, and head the car to the East: *Toledo, Cleveland, New York.*

"Dorothea in the water, all right," Margaretta says. "You can see it with her – there's no such thing as background. Background is what people push aside, when they stick themselves in the center."

Margaretta throws her arm out. Dust on the dashboard rises in an arc and settles on her forearm. "The question," she says, "is how to keep everything shoulder to shoulder, in the foreground. Be democratic about this. Weed stalks, dead, yeah, but right here with you. Asphalt. Fog. And I don't mean pretty scenery! I mean the worm in the flour, the dung on the ground, of any animal you can name, the shit in the water of all the goddamned fish."

Margaretta hands me some crumpled, stained papers. "Here you go. Read through Toledo. Twenty/twenty vision isn't everything. The dead and done-for don't rely on the eyeball."

Confessio in Conversation
— by S. Campbell

From where Confessio stood and farted, two things were clear: what was was no good; and what stunk stunk fine.
He had altered his life, from

fish to fowl already, and had anticipated, with the measured exchange of fin for wing, and now for mind, that good would come of it.

Jonasine warned him not to say anything. "Succumb," she said, "to the temptation to say _nothing_. Because for every word that goes out, three or four come back, out of other mouths, and you have to answer again, and the noise, my god, it spits and hacks around your ears and over your head like fireworks. If you've made some changes," she said, "shut up about it. Nobody needs to know where you've been."

"It's not where I've been I want to talk about," Confessio said, "it's what's in my head, now that it's human, haired."

They were undercover, cloud cover,

mists in the bowels of the whale,
such as they were, tunnels, hills
and dales.

Confessio stretched to his full
height, the attitude of crowing,
but his voice was mild, "Look.
Where's the good?"

Jonasine had no trouble with
that. She pointed to his hair.
"That's good. Your hips, especially,
those are good. You're looking too
far afield."

They were underfire, however.
Clearly enemy fire, in an unusual
skirmish, a chunk of flesh ripped
from the whale wall nearest
Jonasine, small arms fire, and
Confessio dropped to the ground,
hands locked behind his head.
Jonasine crouched low.

"See what I mean!" Confessio
shouted. "Body-build and shitass
pleasures like that, the small
things, pleasure in the small

things, that's what we're about to lose here. Where's the good?"

They were underground, insofar as that was possible, muscle bundles lifted like sod, blanketed back down on them. Jonasine said, "I'd rather argue with you on a back porch. There's no way to prove anything here."

"Well, this is where we are, hey. If you can't prove what you think here, it's no good."

They were underwater, same as always, so deep, it was the truth. "Listen, it's a miracle we're breathing here, you and me," Confessio said. "Why deny what's what?"

"Oh, Confessio," Jonasine said. "Your questions advance your beauty!"

Confessio was irritated. "Look," he said. He pulled his penis out of his pants. "This is still a

pleasure I've got. But so what?
A war's going on, we're the same
as drowned, there's no pasta and
no citrus, nobody's going to visit
and bring news, a fucking body
isn't of any consequence in the
overview of things."

Jonasine saw the paradox in
his thinking as she watched
him, rubbing his penis to
prove a point, perhaps. She
didn't question the proof, the
fiery semen, watery, cloudy,
arcing directly at her — she
raised her hands, not to shield
herself, but to catch what she
could.

They both seemed to feel much
better. They sat around, in the
shelter of the whale. Jonasine
ran her fingers through her
hair. Confessio confessed, "I
know, I read that, too. It's
very good for the hair."

Jonasine sighed. "So much looks so good," she said, "even here." And she meant it, stuck as she was, in the midst of flesh and rapid-fire fire, fumes, and the undetermined fathoms of water weight, outside the walls.

MARGARETTA says, "There it is. I've seen enough to know you can't see in the mind." Margaretta believes what she sees on a page.

WHICH MEANS, of course, Margaretta takes a person's words, like *relics* – those teeth, threads, hairs of Jesus, saved, tended, visible, magical, fraudulent or not – another thing she can get her hands on.

BY THE TIME we cross the Maumee, flat and mud-thick, at Toledo, we've heard the whole Caruso tape, and I've heard the pure contralto tones of Margaretta's voice. She hums, and then she sings, two octaves down. Her voice comes in, with phrases that take a wringing-out-of-the-heart turn upward, and up again. Margaretta knows the words. She holds the notes. She shakes her head, chin up, her black hair swaying sideways, so slow. Mimi!

It's still early March, and Margaretta wears her long brown wool coat. With the heater going, air blowing through the car, we have the fragrant, unassimilated smells of summer pasture – the wool, her hair, fish from the skin of her hands, a vague and distant smell of muck. We're transporting one climate through another. Outside the car, beside the car, fields move by frozen solid in brown trapezoids, with strips of snow along the hedgerows. The sky is antique, winter white.

"Anything that's green out there, we'll see it," Margaretta says. "We'll follow the water until we see some green, it'll have to be your green leaves."

IT IS STRANGE to be with a woman conducting herself in daily, above-ground ways. Margaretta flicks on the turn signal and pulls off into a rest area on the turnpike.

She buys a paper. She opens a wallet, casually. She's used to it. She looks around.

We sit down and Margaretta orders two cups of coffee. She notices people, the waitress in her green uniform.

"Do they buy you that uniform?" Margaretta asks her.

Yes, they do. And when the waitress walks away, Margaretta says, "It is no benefit to a person, ever, to wear a uniform."

At the booth across the aisle, a group of boys is crammed in, drinking Pepsis. One holds a football pennant – green and blue and black – he traces the stiff white lettering, absently, while the boy beside him punches the air, pouf, pouf. They laugh at everything.

Margaretta calls across, "You guys got a girl on your team?"

And then Margaretta leans back and waits for the comments, which hit more or less all at once: "Hell, no!" "Yeah, man, they sit on the bench!" "With their legs crossed, yeah!"

Margaretta hisses, her white teeth all showing. She sips her coffee, and turns to the paper, she opens it to the editorial page and, she's not pretending, she reads the editorials.

ONE OF THE BOYS' chaperones, or coaches, it's hard to say, taps Margaretta on the shoulder. The man leans down as if he's reading an article in the paper. "How far are you driving?" he asks her.

"Pennsylvania," she says. "Why?"

"Are you going to Carlisle?"

"Are we going to Carlisle?" Margaretta asks me.

"We go past there."

"How about if I ride along? I'll give you five bucks."

Margaretta says, "What's your name?"

The man points to his jacket, and written in yellow threading is *Joseph Blue*. His fingers are long, like a pianist's, the nails clean.

"How will you get back?" Margaretta asks, and I begin to see it is fine with her if he rides along. She treats him as if he knows what he's doing.

"I got a girlfriend in Carlisle," Joseph Blue says. He pushes his fingers through his hair, short on the top, bristly, and long on the sides, to his shoulders. Touching his hair would be touching two men, the clipped one and the soft one.

I think, with this thought, it is Margaretta's thought, too. Her hand lifts from the newspaper and rises upward. Then she floats it off to the side, sets it down, palm flat on the tabletop.

ON THE ROAD aimed East, I have discovered this: having subsumed, or been subsumed, for so long, by elemental namesakes, it is no trouble for me to travel, mile after mile, with the ground going by. I'm at home on the move, with a comfort and, maybe thanks to Jack, yes, I guess you could call it, transparency. I'm a soul-to-the-side of Margaretta. She's the one to talk to, because she's the first one to talk. The less I'm attended to, the better I'm able to attend. Sidekicks are the ones who write things down. Does that make Dorothea sidekick to me? She's off somewhere, guessing where I am, writing the pages that might not last until I'm back, if it rains, or floods.

Think of the pages, worldwide, under rocks, layers, whole sedimentary strata, chronicling travels, knifings, hairdos, the trips to Pennsylvania, Budapest, Easter Island, walks across the vacant lot, across mud, down the footpath into the channel.

MARGARETTA reads. She doesn't write.

"*Kiss of the Spider Woman*," Margaretta tells Joseph Blue, "is the title of a book, one of my favorite books. But if you think about it, that's the title of *every* book, right? Kiss of the Fill-in-the-blank Woman! Fish Woman. Word Woman. Kiss of the Chrome-Alloy Woman!"

Joseph Blue pushes his hair behind his ears.

That's how it goes with Margaretta, when she talks, you dive in, and it's no good predicting where you'll come out. She is smart, but she doesn't think things through. She thinks with the muscles around her eyes, with her knees. What she knows and takes for granted is a realm of knowledge dismissed, or unrecognized, by the powers-that-be.

It's apparent, on the turnpike with her, that equations have shifted their terms. You look for the equals sign, it is not where you expect. In measures of wisdom, for instance, youth equals age. No less, no more.

They match. Joseph Blue is a bigwig. In measures of success, in her book, fishmonger equals CEO. Is greater than, to be blunt.

You see why, in a restaurant, or on the turnpike, the plainest, least controversial details loom suddenly into focus as grotesque distortions, abuses of power. And the air reels out of balance, the weather is in a constant state of collapse, rain around one corner, then backstage scrims of fog, or bedazzled sun and wind. And houses collect like huts, airplanes like foreign missiles, for god's sake. Signs, billboards, the most ordinary things, now they are revelations, the notations of monied madmen. Fences, something simple as that, she will point out as meshed, home-spun markers of fear.

Margaretta hollers to truckers, "Where are the women?" At Cadillacs, she shouts, "Where are the insects, my god, where is the dust and dirt!"

Margaretta wants everything visible.

Riding is smooth, but her talk isn't. These are wholesale destructions Margaretta sets in motion.

WHEN SHE'S GOING on, all this calamity and exhilaration, I lean back. I stretch out my legs on the backseat, and I arrange for myself a clear picture: Margaretta, her black hair, and the handsaw on the nail. The teeth of the saw, the stamp of the manufacturer's name on the blade. The carved-out grip in the wood handle, the steel nail bent like a hook, the wood wall.

A handsaw on a nail. It's not in the background, not behind her, but on the wall, there at her shoulder. Right there.

MARGARETTA harangues Joseph Blue, who is reading the newspaper, his head propped against the window. "The news should be one thing after another," she says, "that's it. On TV, unedited sound. *All* the pictures."

She says a camera should be mounted on a car – a cheap Horizon, I suppose – and run continuously. The car would just keep driving overland, then be ferried across water, in the hold of a ship, the camera still running down there – you'd see black for a while – that's what you'd watch, and then all the stops across Africa for gas, to buy food, crossing borders, the camera would reel on and on. Across Egypt or the Sudan. Through the Middle East, no specials on the military or the oil, no specials on anything. On the concrete steps of a house, no trees around, you'd see three boys in shorts. You'd hear a voice shout, Where are the girls? Where are the rooted plants, the fish?

"IF YOU WANT to see the fish, fish not caught, you have to go underwater," I interject.

THE WEATHER inside the car complicates our travel. The coffee-to-go and the words out of Margaretta's mouth fill the open spaces, uprising spirals from the coffee, and out of Margaretta's mouth – words like *where* and *fish* appear cloudlike, they are visible words, with distinct shapes, until they disperse in the car.

We are balmy with fogs in this car, past Youngstown and on towards Pittsburgh. Near the Pennsylvania line, the East becomes apparent, with its groomed trees closer to the road, although there is no leafing yet, whole hillsides of houses, the mass constructions in coal towns, and then in the hills outside Pittsburgh, ledges and overhang housing, up the sideslopes, with the calculated rooflines, one so close to another, that mean – well, you know what they are meant to mean. Jobs, homes, boom time, boom. Not – no, no! – scars, gashes, dirt dollars.

"Jesus Christ goddamnit," Margaretta swears. "Dorothea didn't buy her place, did she? They didn't *develop* her slot of water, did they?"

I don't know how Dorothea fits into the economy.

"No," I say. "She didn't pay for the place in the channel."

I'm at a loss. My feet go cold, then damp. Dorothea washes over me, she floods my mind, and I have the sensation of flailing, then clambering onto high spots, to hang on for a while. My feet have that feet-of-clay feel, sinking, slogging, they slide from the seat of the car. Dorothea strolls, water woman, and I recognize the rankness, the wet grass and ground smell, that penetrates my hair and covers my skin, a sheen of water cells, inside to outside, outside to inside. With Dorothea, bodily definition is not by outline-able shape, epidermal cells, but by intracellular fluid – the water body itself stands there and flows, unconfined.

"You see, that makes sense," Margaretta says, in her fish-cleaver voice. "Water is priceless. Dorothea knows that. Anybody knows that. And so, goddamnit, should be all the *dirt*!"

"You know," Joseph Blue says, "When I was in Mongolia, arable land was so rare, nobody was allowed to own it. You paid a fee, like rent, to use it."

"Mongolia?" Margaretta asks.

She swings her head back towards me. Her hair sweeps around her neck, like a full skirt.

WE'RE ON the Allegheny Plateau of Pennsylvania, across the globe from Mongolia, through the core – with a long way downslope to go.

Joseph Blue, no doubt about it, has talked his way cross-country before. He is in the right car – Margaretta, with her blistered elbows, is an audience designed for rapt attention, who else would say, "So? What about Mongolia?"

Joseph Blue talks, and his hands meet in front of his chest. His hands fall, circle in air, clench, fold. He pushes his hair, he claps his hands when he laughs. Or he frowns, he scratches his arms slowly, cracks his knuckles, crosses his arms. This is not nervousness, but the visible conducting of narration – its syncopations, difficult measures, the more assured recaps through the codas, tunnel to tunnel through the midsection of the turnpike.

IF YOU ASK Joseph Blue what happened, and you know Margaretta does, he tells you. Is it too much or too little?

He starts with his dirt farmer days in Mongolia, when he paid rent for a plot of ground behind a hinge factory. These were ordinary hinges for cupboard doors, he says, small metal hinges, the first ones manufactured and sold into China. Tillable ground, as you know now, was so rare in those days that anything with some clay or loam in it, anything not the color of desert, even if it was dirt in the back lot of a factory, was up for grabs. Joseph Blue noticed a mustard-yellow dhreena flowering – an indication the ground was fertile – in a corner near a discarded packing crate. He signed up for that plot, paid the use fee. Joseph Blue was not Joseph Blue then, but Rwalda Dhramu.

Joseph Blue's fingers tap the sides of his chest.

I N   F O U R   P A R T S

He kept a sand-colored dog, Leht, in his living room, this was extravagance, yes, but he trained the dog, or the dog had a natural talent, Joseph Blue cannot be sure of this—it ferreted out the moles in their tunnels under the eggplants, it stalked the gray-haired rodents that concealed themselves in the greens of chard. Joseph Blue owned two tools, a hoe and a kema, something like a spade, but much more pointed, razor-sharp.

If you ask Joseph Blue what year this was, he's not sure.

He is sure about the hinge factory, the hoe and the kema, the dog Leht.

His recollection of weather is finely detailed. He remembers the springtime dust in the air, and the red-chalk taste of it. He can explain how, before sunset, the colors of the sky arranged themselves horizontally, indigo on top, then several less solid blues, followed by two or three stripes of orange-gold, then a thick white line, like a wall of mist, along the ground.

Joseph Blue's hands arrange the colors.

He says what created the display was the Gobi desert and suspended particles in the air, floating predictably, the dead calm between five and seven. If you ask him about his family, if he had a family, he's not sure. He tells you about the calm between five and seven, and about the eggplant he cooked, seasoned with hot red peppers and a yellow bean paste. He says, "Oh yes, there was a goose in the hinge factory, as its guard."

If you ask Joseph Blue what language he spoke, he will say, "The language of that place." If you say to him, and Margaretta does, "Well, since you remember the word kema, what other words do you remember?"

he'll say, "The *kema* cut off two of my fingers, I could never forget, and I also remember *dhreena*, the yellow flowering plant. The word for goose I do not remember."

Joseph Blue leans back. Margaretta says, "I'll be damned."

Joseph Blue continues his account and describes the African lake of another childhood. Along the edges of this lake grew a peculiar red algae, so that the lake appeared purplish viewed from the village slope. Joseph Blue says that lake-purple is a color he rarely sees anywhere in this country, but when he does see it, in fabric most often, he buys a yard or two and hangs these pieces on a clothesline, where the wind shakes them – it is almost watery.

Joseph Blue describes the lake smell, rank and sweet, like a cellar with peaches, some of them overripe. Birds were attracted to the lake, especially the Harga cranes in migration. He says he liked to lie in the hollow trunk of a fallen tree when the cranes flew in, thousands, overhead. They circled in approach, then let themselves fall, their wings sideways, they plummeted, but they caught themselves at the last minute, and directly over the tree, they set their wings wide, like fans, for the glide in. The long gray legs trailed. Air rushed through the feathers of their wings, wwh – wh – whh.

He blows this air through his teeth.

Joseph Blue recalls the soup his mother made from nuts and the spinachlike leaves of *sunga*. If you ask him about his mother he'll tell you she was tall, with a rich operatic voice – his name in that place, Lladla, was musical when she spoke it. She died of an infection, her eyes glaucous, sunk in the shadow of her brow, although he nursed her for two weeks, and even sang to her.

In that village it was the custom to carve geometric shapes in a boy's face, precise knife-cuts all over the face, and Joseph Blue mentions how, even now, he jumps back when his girlfriend reaches sometimes to touch his face.

Go ahead, ask him about a father, or sisters and brothers, he cannot say. If you ask him about the denominations of currency, or the shapes of houses, or how he himself died, he is not sure. Joseph Blue makes no apologies for these lapses. Or for the continuities of his accounts – he will tell you: "What I remember, I remember well."

AND YOU'RE LEFT with a problem – how to think about what he says – that isn't much different from the problem you'd have with any-one else's recollections, even your own.

MARGARETTA asks Joseph Blue, "Were you ever a woman?"

"It's hard to say," he says. He was born so many times, he explains, in so many places that a vision of the birth canal – a wormhole, uncoiling in brilliant colors, with the widening darkness of space like a door at the exit – appears to him several times a day, vivid, it is not like a dream, whenever he dozes off.

He wonders if, as a woman, he could have given birth to himself.

WHEN A PERSON can't fill out a simple questionnaire – and how could Joseph Blue? – you can ask anything you want.

IT IS POSSIBLE Joseph Blue's love of various climates has kept him going, it does not seem to be a matter of spirit, or reincarnation. He has nothing to say on spiritual subjects, nothing at all. He's a body in one place and one time, and then he's a body in another. Apparently, this is a human issue, exclusively. He has not been a reptile, or insect, or succulent plant. If you ask, he says, "I am always just somebody walking around."

Right now, he is walking around Morenci, Michigan. Margaretta asks what he'll remember from there, and he says, "Well, it could be the weed field." He describes the pattern of white Queen Anne's lace, and chicory, blue through late summmer, and then the sequence of coneflowers, milkweed, goldenrod, purple aster. She asks which name of that bunch he'll remember. "Milkweed," he says. He laughs and you see the large creases on his face. He'll kid around this way, but he is serene, not false in his confidences. He says he likes the smell of basil so much, he's sure that will stick.

At thirty-five, Joseph Blue claims to own very little. He has objects inside and outside his house, he says, clothes, a telephone, his girlfriend Lucy in Carlisle, who is so young, she is only ten, he's not sure the match will have time to work.

"Ten?" Margaretta exclaims. "Ten!"

Joseph Blue says that Lucy thinks she was a bird at one time, but he says, "You know how that is, the way kids like to imagine things, she's a smart kid." He'll hold his judgment on all of that, he says, until she's older. He says Lucy has a singing voice like his mother's, and if you ask, as Margaretta does, "Do you mean your mother now or the one in Mongolia?" he catches you right away and says, "I mean Africa." He says it wouldn't surprise him if there *was* a connection to Lucy. It's crossed his mind, he says, that Lucy could be his mother. "That could be," he admits. "Nothing wrong with that, it would be a different gene pool entirely, we'd just be close."

THIS IS AS CRAZY, I would guess, as Joseph Blue gets.

JOSEPH BLUE drives truck for a hay broker. He has a garden – eggplants, Roma tomatoes – and he visits Lucy whenever he has time off, and money for gas. He is sure he'll remember the electric lines along Route 20, the poles fifty feet tall, an ancient pine forest skinned for this project, each pole a triple-crossed T. When fog accumulates in the low spots, he says, the poles rise directly out of it, like uprooted things, miraculously balanced.

If you ask Joseph Blue about the future, he says, "It's easier to see than to change." He says, "I'm a Democrat, I haven't got investments in the future." He adds, "I believe I'm a pacifist, too." He says when he was a dirt farmer in Mongolia, he cut off the first two fingers of his left hand, slicing an eggplant. "Violence finds me," he says. "I don't seek it."

He doesn't remember wars, or military attacks, offensive or defensive. He doesn't mention assault, assassination, ambush, torture. Joseph Blue seems to know only the cuts of his own skin.

"That's all I can tell you," he says. He holds up his hands in front of his face, he spreads the fingers apart and looks at Margaretta through them, ten fingers intact – proof of his present, as-yet-unmutilated life.

"I DON'T KNOW, Joseph Blue," Margaretta says. "You got a long and complicated life going for you."

JOSEPH BLUE rolls down the window. "It smells like goat," he says. "I smell goat."

"You smell houses," Margaretta says. "Those are houses out there. You don't smell tobacco from Lancaster County anymore, that's all."

"I think it's a drought," Joseph Blue says.

"Well, it's not flooded, that's for sure. You're right about that."

Those two go at it, reconnoitering the air. The next hundred miles, they attempt to calculate the moisture content of soils, from the interior of the car. But in March, the wetness or dryness of any temperate climate anywhere in the Northern Hemisphere cannot be directly observed, that's how it is, the place is frozen – no greenery, or lack of it, as a measure. They stab at the numbers. They sniff.

THE APPROACH, coming into Carlisle – the descent – is smooth, dulled, out of the Appalachians like clouds, out of the Blue Mountain tunnel where the car sweeps through a curve. And there are the afternoon mists, hung in domestic valleys, the spongy blue-to-bluer hills with the fade-out in the distance to white, the yellow middle-distance where everything *looks* like Pennsylvania – cultivated, clipped, patterned with ready-to-go fields and intervening bulk-built subdivisions. The incidental trees – we're out of the woods – are branched according to subspecies shapes, dark gray, laced.

Joseph Blue swears these are desert-type conditions, he says coyotes will be in backyards. Margaretta chalks up the predator-prey scent, which she doesn't deny, to overdevelopment and the loss of cover.

SOMEWHERE around here, I kick my feet out of my shoes. Somewhere around here, the watershed shifts.

A divide shunts rainwater into the east-flowing Susquehanna, and now we're facing the Atlantic. Not the Gulf, by way of the Mississippi, not the St. Lawrence Seaway by way of the Great Lakes.

And now this happens, although it is not raining – this probably is a drought – there's a pull, a graver, new gravity in my feet, and Joseph Blue's convoluted talk, flowing and turbulent as floodwater, all those ages and places in one voice, wash over me, wash – and I'm out of there, carried down and out, no slam of the car door, a liquid blackout – the way, when the body faints, for instance, a blackness edges in, and the fizz and itch in the cells warn about loss to come.

It is the action of shutdown, defiant laws that, in a persistent state, sustain Dorothea, against all odds, submerged. I am immediately out of range of transportation. S. has assumed her extraordinary powers, she's infiltrated again, surfaced.

WE WASH OUT. Down. Below. We're in shallow waters, clear, silvery-slim as minnows, the stream is full of them. We follow the current, I doubt this is swimming proper, the muscles don't move but find their way. The body – think of it this way – streamlined, shoulder to toe, takes its bygone place in water, buoyed on all sides. The upright hierarchy loses sway. Downstream, and farther, we are headed on with the head-first knowledge that this stream will flow to another, the astoundingly small gradations in level, laser-accurate, leading the double hydrogen and simple oxygen atoms on and on – we stream with the stream. Has S. learned to latch onto oxygen wherever she finds it, is that it? There is no struggle in the breathing, no struggle at all.

The various landscapes and bridges, magnified by water, shaken by it, roll past like fast film. Water is so much smoother than air. Air is conglomerate, a mixture, and the body must take it in, always in and out, sorting the oxygen, working the lungs. But with S., in her element, hair flowing back, the cells are in repose. If the body somersaults, or nose forward, twirls around, cylindrically, the backbone suffers no pressures. In the watery calms, the vertebrae click, separate, the muscles ease, and there is so much room for the bones now within the skin.

What a way to travel, downslope, out of the Appalachians. We're cascading down a spillway. The network of tributaries, that-a-way, branching down, linking eastward, closer through packets of rapids, every skid, to the trunk of the Susquehanna.

MARGARETTA, she'll put two and two together, she's smart enough to find fish – she'll find us. But what will she do with Joseph Blue?

UNDERWATER, things are not what you think. There is no confusion, first of all, no one-way traffic, no solid or dotted lines, your sense of direction is exact, irrefutable, whether you go with the current or against it, whether you cut at right angles to it, or sit stock-still, footed in mud, clammed shut. This is a lost and found knowledge, the assurance of touch, head to foot. This is buoyancy, hazard, and waywardness – what it is to be at home, unhoused, ongoing. Elsewhere, alert, you have to admit, nothing surrounds you, not air, no, it's out of hand. We've pushed it off, walled it in, walled it out. However it once was for a person's body, moving around, when it was creaturely, thoughtless, is a recollection that comes back only in lapses, when we lose track – in lovemaking when it is ranging, sweated, benumbed; or when we fall on the ground as children, dizzy from spinning, and feel the ground under us, careening.

There is comfort in the collapse upon the planet. Upon another body. There is no other comfort without delusion. In water, you remember lovemaking, if you have made love, and dancing in circles if you have danced in circles. And that's about it, for memory.

THE ENORMOUS interest in things, underwater. Shells of freshwater clams, some open, some shut, and the layers of twigs, leaves, preserved in their colors, at the foot of rocks in pools. We are as interesting here as fish! Hair is a spectacle, nails on the toes and feet, like shells, or a version of scales, they are so unusual. Think of the water plants, wildly adapted with floating saucer leaves, fringed stalks, segmented. Look at Dorothea, now, open-eyed, her swimming legs not far from the motions of fin, her pubic hair wiry, a patch of waterweed.

Downstream, with us, the snub-nosed fish, fish with eye rings like bull's-eyes, the iridescence of trout, crayfish in lulls, pivoting, quick, cumbersome. S. takes charge. We surge through some shallows. Hemlocks on shore, woods of them, darken the water. Then the stream widens, deepens, a pall of smoke from a shack on the shore interferes with light filtering down, we are coming close to a town, more houses, white squares, floating, peripheral, and docks jutted at angles, and tires, cans, the town floor of a waterway now.

S. aims herself underwater, like a missile. She zeroes in on the channels, cuts corners.

Where the stream merges with the Juniata River, I recognize three things overhead: a bridge I have crossed, a stone bridge, arched slightly, peculiarly; a rock formation, remarkable even through water, overhanging the river, the face of a goat, some say, or the face of God, it depends what you call the rocks on top, halo or horns; and then, clearer than any of these, out in the middle of the river, a brick tower, some remnant, crumbling. A fort? An old bridge? We pass it, and I know the way from here.

The Juniata to Clark's Ferry, this won't take long–and there, we merge with the Susquehanna, the blue water, blue-arm, blue-barrel, blue air, blue hair, last long route to travel.

Mountains fall to the Susquehanna, down suddenly, like gates it has swung through, all the way to Harrisburg. S. is a blur through these waters, I wouldn't have believed she could travel so fast. The water absorbs different smells, local, with each bend in the river, the various influxes of effluents, tar near the railroad yards, or creosote, sulfurs, chlorines, silts, fertilizers, soaps, and the sweeter, yes, you'd have to say sweeter, smells of human waste. The water, reflective of none of this, within itself grows full, laden. There's more work to swimming, although it is not the weight of the water that's changed, it's watery as ever, but the feel of it, more slippery, the smell of it, the look from the bottom up, slows us down.

Past Harrisburg, past Middletown–Three Mile Island–the travel goes more and more slowly, but evenly, steadily. We approach our exit, Columbia, where the river stretches out, becalms itself, a mile across, sprawled among room-size rocks, flat as floors. This is the jumping-off point, one of those rooms.

MARGARETTA will recognize the place. She knows the bridge, she knows the rocks. She'll stop the car, look around until she spots us, and then she'll wave both arms in the air, cross them, cross them, a signal, in case we need one.

WHO NEEDS ONE? She's there. Out of the blue boxcar. How many minutes, hours has it been?

Margaretta, just herself, Joseph Blue is elsewhere. Is he reunited with his girlfriend Lucy in Carlisle? Are there isles in Carlisle? I guess yes.

Margaretta, out there, surveying the unwalled stone rooms of the river, yells something.

The wind blows her hair out at the sides like a tent, a veil. From here, she looks like a woman in mourning, black net over the face, swathed around the head. But the wind switches, her hair flies up, and her wide face, the drawn-in shapes of her eyes, open up, her teeth part.

I FIND my shoes in the car.

Dried off, on land, leaning on the hood, I'm set. The world looks clearer, of course, out of water. S. is in decline. She's back in the water cells, that's how it feels, the fluid cells in the thighs, is that it? She has no idea of the purpose of the trip; she is propellent, that's all. She cushions, she reposes, she shuts her eyes, all potential, the half-moon under the nail, the wet underside of the tongue, lips, labia, labyrinthian recesses, she's the fluid connection where nerves end. She's the lull, the zap.

"BABE, you missed a family scene!" Margaretta says. She pulls out a Thermos of coffee, two mugs stamped with a highway map and the words The Original Turnpike, USA. She has frequented another rest stop, that's what it looks like. She could pick up a ride – did she? – wherever she stopped. Margaretta is freewheeling, out on the road. She is public transportation.

"You missed Carlisle," she says.

We sit on the hood of the car and overlook the Susquehanna, green and yellow shadows wavering between the rocks.

Margaretta opens up her maps.

I point to a blank area, the one blank area, in the shape of a capital D on the county map. "That's about where the springhouse was."

"X marks the watercress," Margaretta says. She draws an X in the D.

The map is crowded with roads, the hatching of urban boundaries, Lancaster sprawling, its yellow extensions covering Centerville, formerly no place, and Blue Ball on Route 30, that's swallowed up, too.

"You missed Carlisle," Margaretta says again. "Listen, I don't know what to tell you, except to tell you. There's no one thing. You know what I mean?"

MARGARETTA says it was easy. Easy off the turnpike into Carlisle, Joseph Blue directing – onto South Steet, no wrong turns, a street north, paradoxically, of Main. And attached to the post office there, brick wall to wall, second floor up, Joseph Blue knocked, knock, knock, knock.

Opening the door, there was Lucy Del Laraine, ten years old, one hand pushing the doorframe, one hand landing on her head. She yelled, "Hurray!"

Joseph Blue clapped his hands. And then he did this, Margaretta says. He fell to his knees, down on his elbows, most devout. Margaretta gasped. But then she swallowed that, and said, "All right, but how will you gallop at seventy-five?" Because Joseph Blue was not, in fact, devout, he had made himself into a horse for the entertainment of Lucy.

And Lucy jumped on his back, threw her arms in the air. She called "Aunt Charlaine!" and they rode inside.

Lucy and her Aunt Charlaine, it was her great-aunt, Margaretta says, laid claim to a place as murky, apparently, as Dorothea's water-hole. The apartment was unlighted. It was a three-room apartment, room one, room two, room three, with one window, a small window, high on the wall over a sink. Charlaine Del Laraine, well, good god, Margaretta says, in two steps she was across the room, she was tall, with heavy white hair piled, coiled, on top of her head. She wore a purple terry cloth robe, and Margaretta's opinion is, she was out of place in a dark place. Aunt Charlaine should have been on a ledge in sunlight, Margaretta says, somewhere with blasts of overheated air, the Mediterranean, the Moroccan coast. Mesa Verde, on top of red rocks. But no, she was in Carlisle. Fine wrinkles like bones, opaque fishbones, that's her face.

"Who are you?" Aunt Charlaine said to Margaretta.

Margaretta said, "I brought Joseph Blue."

"And now, I suppose, you'll take us away," Aunt Charlaine said. And here she reached into the pocket of her robe and pulled out a gold-plated revolver, a gold gun. Okay, was it a cigarette lighter? Margaretta thought it was. Aunt Charlaine held the gun like a skillet, in front of her belly, easy in her hand as if she was ready to cook.

She said, "Lucy goes nowhere." She sat on an orange sofa and propped her feet on a table.

Margaretta sat down, too. She says, since the migrant camp in Coatesville, she's carried a knife. Always. But Margaretta kept that fact to herself. She says she took her time, she sat down.

From where she sat, she could see an unattached leg of a fly, she says that's what it was—a fine-hewn thing, a snipped, thread-jointed leg of a fly—on a piece of white paper by Aunt Charlaine's foot.

The paper had nothing written on it. It glowed, in the room where nothing was lighted. Aunt Charlaine's revolver, too, looked lit up—it burned holes, or filled them, in space when it moved in her hand. She moved the gun hand-to-hand.

This is what there was in the room to look at: the paper and the gun. Everything else, Margaretta had to guess at.

Everything else—orange sofa, the chair where Margaretta sat, a folding chair, rugs, walls—where were they? Margaretta says this was like the vision she remembered as a kid, when she looked so hard at one thing that it pulsated and ballooned itself, expanded like a sun going supernova, while other points left to right slipped from focus. The empty paper or the golden gun, it doesn't matter which, distorted absolutely, and applied itself, like the mother-of-pearl of cataracts, to the whole eye. If you looked at Margaretta's eyeballs, there, see, she says, there were no eyeballs at all, you'd have seen white paper circles or gold gun circles. She says this has nothing to do with being afraid. She is talking about what a person sees, and how.

I N   F O U R   P A R T S

How many places are there where, if you look, point blank, you see the leg of a fly on white paper at Aunt Charlaine's feet and a gun in Aunt Charlaine's hand? A couple of places, I'd say. More than you'd like to think, according to Margaretta.

In a minute or so, at the doorway of room two, Joseph Blue appeared, upright, Lucy riding high on his shoulders, holding onto his hair at the sides, like reins. Lucy ducked. Her head nearly hit the doorframe. They jabbered – catching up on news: Lucy told about her fifth-grade science project. She called Joseph Blue, Blue. "Blue, where've you been?" They walked around the orange sofa.

He said, "I drove the truck to Arkansas."

"What do you think you're doing?" Aunt Charlaine said.

"I'm talking to Lucy," Joseph Blue said. "We could get some pizza. How about if we do that?"

"Lucy goes nowhere," said Aunt Charlaine.

"Fine. That's fine. They'll deliver. I'm not going anywhere either," Joseph Blue said. He bent down, Lucy jumped free, and they walked into room two to find the phone.

Margaretta, she was all right by this time. A Carlisle world of children and guns and possible abduction, well it was foreign to fishery, except it was dark and it put a watery pressure on the lungs. She folded her hands behind her neck, a headrest, and she sat in the folding chair the way she sat in a car, eyes forward, body relaxed, in the midst of things. She looked at Aunt Charlaine and said nothing.

Lucy, at the doorway, said, "Extra cheese?"

Aunt Charlaine put the gun in her pocket. "Sure, extra cheese," she said. "Do you want a drink?" she asked Margaretta.

"A glass of water," Margaretta said. She stood up, walked towards room two. "I'll get it."

Other places in Carlisle, Margaretta says, anybody knows it, you could find houses with dining-room tables, bedspreaded beds – like stage sets, with the usual families sitting – you could find these things without too much trouble. But not here.

Margaretta sat down with a cup of water.

On the sofa, Lucy showed Joseph Blue her art class drawings – finger paintings, with finger marks, curled in blue waves, red prints from the thumb, pulled through the water, four of the red prints drawn together, anemonelike, water flowers under water, there was no source of light, but the colors appeared in their own color-generated lights, dark blue, red water-rooted thumb flowers.

Joseph Blue said, "Beautiful. Lovely." He took a pencil, and on the blank paper with the fly leg, he drew Lucy a picture of the pizza he'd ordered.

"Well, goddamnit, Joseph Blue," Margaretta said, "that looks like a bloodshot eye. Good for you." She encouraged him, she says, because he was not true-to-life – how could he be? – not bound to a well-lit realism and its requirements: the plates under pizzas, for instance, the tables under the plates, the floors under tables, and so on. The sphere of Joseph Blue's pizza obeyed no laws of two-dimensional space, or three, no laws of gravity. It hung there in pencil on the page.

In Carlisle, Margaretta claims, Lucy participated in a suspension, too, corralled in the dark with Aunt Charlaine, tethered to Joseph Blue, who knows how.

IT'S CLEAR Margaretta has a talent possibly akin to fish-filleting. She finds flesh, the interior bodily caverns, gall, liver, lung, she gets to it. Past the last rib, where the knife can slip under and clear the abdominal cavity.

Joseph Blue smells goat in sunlight, but Margaretta sees in the dark. He nosed her out! But she saw right through him. How else could she end up in Carlisle? A stopover suitable – it was rudimentary enough – for Dorothea, Jean-Paul, Jack, all together.

It was so dark, Margaretta says, she could turn her head, look off-sides, and see *better*, the way in a room at night you look at the edges to see what you want to see.

LUCY READ her homework to Margaretta, a paragraph on the spotted salamander. Margaretta sat on the chair and drank the water.

"I found one in there," Lucy said. She meant spotted salamander, and she pointed to room one.

"You have a scientific eye," Margaretta said. "I found a fish in a fish one time. A bass, not too big, with a bluegill down its throat. Whole. Both of them."

"Did you eat them both?" Lucy asked.

"I sold them both. Fish in a fish, like this." Under the floating pizza, Margaretta drew scales and fins, tooth and tail, one inside one, a version of what she'd seen. Lucy looked over her shoulder, one hand in Margaretta's hair.

Aunt Charlaine said, "The fish is bad at the Carlisle Family Restaurant. It's disgusting," she said. "Well, it's not that, it's not the food, it's the words, *family restaurant*. I won't go. If you don't look like mother and father – who does here? – or mother and daughter – well, if you are your own self, or old lady in her robe and Lucy, well, how can we sit there and eat the chicken and bad fish."

"Halibut," Lucy said. "Blue and I go there."

"When was this?" Aunt Charlaine said.

"Last summer. Nobody paid attention. We ate dinner."

Joseph Blue said, "I look like her uncle. It doesn't bother me."

"Blend in, then," Aunt Charlaine said.

"Well, she does look related," Joseph Blue said.

"I know she does. So what? That's my point. No reason in the world people should look related. I like those Whoever's-Out-There-Come-In Restaurants. Or the We-Deliver places. Pizza's a wonderful thing, see, they deliver it, or you can go in and eat it, or you take it out, it doesn't matter. It's not a native thing, and any sort of American can eat it."

"It's good cold," Lucy said.

"We eat it for breakfast," Aunt Charlaine said.

Joseph Blue settled back on the floor, his head propped against the sofa. Aunt Charlaine sat, as she had been sitting, on the sofa, feet up on the plank coffee table. Beside her, Lucy rocked forward and backward.

Margaretta, opposite, looked at them.

With a flash for illumination, Margaretta says, this would have made a good picture – the orange sofa, the purple robe, Joseph Blue's dual-cut hair, Lucy in motion, blurred.

"YOU COULD draw it," I tell Margaretta.

But I know what she has in mind – she'd like to hand me something, as souvenir, something cheap, a whim, something partial, inaccurate, half-glimpsed. She wants to say, "There's no one thing I can tell you. Look. This proves it."

THE STREAM is not where it should be. Not in the blank space of the D. There is no blank. Houses, a new crossroad.

"What do you think?" Margaretta asks. "Do you think it's buried?"

We've followed the map, into Lancaster County, where roads are re-routed, although that in itself would not be an obstacle to finding a stream, some nosing around would turn up the recognizable hills, the hill with the hawk nose, the hill with the dome-top rock. But in addition to reroutings, new roads, new hills have been constructed and others planed down, to allow for placement of, as you read on the signs, executive homes. Maps can't keep up, no scale is large enough to include the Orchard Lanes and the cul-de-sac Meadow Courts that lie on all the hill-sides.

Nonetheless, Margaretta asks at a Party Store and we find our way, in a general way, to the midpoint between Mountville and Mount Joy – points A and B – between which had been – for how long? – stream, spring, rock, cress. We pull onto the shoulder of Oyster Point Road, a familiar curve, the name is the same, and I say with assurance, "There."

Well, you know it, it's not there.

MARGARETTA opens the hatch of the Horizon, this happens so fast. She breaks a metal clothes hanger, she bends it back and forth until it snaps, she breaks off the hook, and she stretches the two metal rods out – a water-witching device. She walks away from the road, then parallel to it, she is divining water. A few steps, and she says, "Here."

I see the loosely held rods angle into each other, cross, waver, delicately.

She walks back and forth. The same thing happens each time, the same places.

The water is where it's supposed to be, but buried, storm-sewered.

Does it flood down there? How large must the pipe be, to allow for spring thaws, who makes the calculations, and has the water, during wet years, burst through, I suppose it would, surge to the surface and re-channel itself through the backyards of the executive homes. Do the executives go outside and take pictures of the muddy water swirling under the swingsets?

"Well, water is right here," Margaretta says. "Was the springhouse near this road?"

"About a mile that way, but it's probably piped, right from the source. We'll never find it."

"What about Dorothea?" Margaretta says. "Isn't that what she knows all about?"

I AM ABLE to say, I hear the words, "We know some of the same things."

YES, MY FEET shift, at my say-so, my hair is already wet, and I'm out of my shoes.

At a point Margaretta marks on the ground, where the backyards of the large houses slope together, I raise my arms over my head, close my eyes, and turn around. And keep turning. I circle with the intuitions, the muscle motions of you-know-who, but I have my own intentions.

What does Margaretta see – a blur? S. and Jean-Paul and Jack, that's what I see. Myself. We spiral, we escalate – the fluid meltdown power of S., Jean-Paul's charged, blow-torch hair, Jack's invisibility, his whirlwind collisions and calms.

To go underground, more problematic than diving underwater, there's nothing to do but call on the body in all its parts, fleshed, fisted, lathed, almost metallic – coppery with the tremendous turning. This is ferocity of will, not wish. It takes shape. The bullet body. Dervish body. Deep-sea drill bit. Rocket. Pocket, power packet. Maelstrom. Missile. Heat-seeker, sidewinder. Wrecker ball. Whale jaw. Ripsaw.

I HIT the dirt. And it gives. Not an explosion, but a simple machine-cut, incisive, and fanned from my feet, pulled down with me, a crater, a sinkhole, closed back over, you'd never know a body had hit. The way meteorites penetrate, and bury themselves, slow to cool.

The water's right there. The concrete pipe – a tap of the fist – cracks and body-size chunks fall in, a dam. The water inside rises, backs up. And this part is easy, swimming upstream, upflow, the pipe holds while the water fills, it'll hold for a while. I can swim, keep my head above water.

There is no light, the water is slick with clay, the unsettled silt. I keep going, swimming, long strokes, until the water begins to flow colder over my shoulders – the ice-cut of springwater. My fingertips feel the freeze, they stiffen. There's the scent of cress, in the dark, a suggestion of it. Then the brush of hairlike roots, broken off, flowing past. A root, a long thread, catches across my nose.

The pipe narrows, and here is a tangle of roots, I'm getting close, then – leaves, whole leaves, like lids on the eyes, smooth, cool.

I take a leaf in my mouth like a wafer, and who wouldn't smile.

It's watercress.

Nothing sanctified, nothing sacred – these are leaves. The plant is still growing near the spring, adapted, somehow, to pitch, definitive dark. The watercress won't be green. How could it be? The leaves will be pallid, like bleached lettuces, leaves white as roots.

I can fill my arms with leaves now. Will it grow in light? In the channel?

The pipe narrows so much, it cracks at my shoulders. This is the end of the line.

Arms full of plants, I head upwards, the noise is tremendous, dirt combs through my hair, the ground warms, it is hot to the touch. My hair burns down my back, the top of my head is raw. Then the break, the surprising mushroom of dirt, in the air, a press of oxygen, blistering light – it pours over my skin. I have to close my eyes.

"DELICIOUS!" Margaretta says. She eats a handful of leaves. They are paper-flat, paper white. She takes the cress in big bunches, and fills the buckets. "Great," she says. "How did you find them?"

She hands me a towel, and I sit down on the ground, winter grass, another backyard. I wipe my face. I wrap my head in the towel, like a sultan, and look around. A few people head our way, they pull on coats, some long dark coats, some short ski jackets, a family of coats. From another back door, three more people.

Water collects in the exit hole, where the sod heaves up at peculiar angles. Water seeps down the slopes of this sod, it is headed for a line of clipped barberry, one way, and headed for a blue spruce, planted just right, in a basin, the other way. We are borderline, between properties. Large roofed houses loom upslope, white and brown-trimmed, east and west. We have disturbed two groomed lawns. Houses rise in the distance, impressive as hills, one behind the other.

A boy approaches, long-legged, he carries a video camera on his shoulder, he is aiming the machine at Margaretta, at the hole in the ground, at me, the towel and the dirt-shoulders. He doesn't come too close, not yet, his family has not yet arrived at his side.

Margaretta packs up. She kicks some chunks of dirt towards the hole, although the water is deep now, a pool.

"What's going on!" calls the father of the boy.

Margaretta helps me up, hands me a bucket to carry, she leads me off the way she must have walked, water-witching, to get here, maybe tracking the tremors.

The boy's father heads back to his house, loping along. But the boy holds the camera on us, distant as we are, it won't be much to see, I'm afraid he'll be disappointed.

"Let's get out of here," Margaretta says.

A man in a ski jacket, across the other way, waves his arms and cuts across the yard at an angle.

We intersect, near the next large house.

"Are you with the state?" he asks. He fingers the fabric of his sleeve.

"No," Margaretta says. "We were tracking down an old spring, for the watercress."

"Do you have cats?" he asks.

"Cats? No," Margaretta says.

"Do you have dogs?" the man asks me. His hair, cut short, sticks out in sprigs from under a black ski cap.

"No, I don't," I say.

"I have a dog. I had a poodle. It died two years ago. I've thought about digging him up, but it wouldn't make any difference, would it? Do you have a picture of your cats?"

"I don't have cats," Margaretta says.

"Do you have any pictures?"

Margaretta sets down the buckets. She is not one to walk away from a conversation. She takes her wallet out of her coat pocket, opens it up, slips out four or five photographs. She hands them over to the man. "They're friends of mine. No cats."

"Who's this?"

"That's Elmer."

"Where's he now?"

"Right now? He's probably in jail."

"Would you write out his name for me?" The man takes a scrap of paper from his jacket, he searches and finds a pencil in his pocket.

"All right," Margaretta says. She writes the name, Elmer Amdek.

"I might run into him sometime, you never know," the man says. He folds the paper carefully.

"Sweetheart," Margaretta says, "we must take this watercress home."

She pushes me ahead of her through the midsection of the development.

Nobody follows. What day is it? Are they asleep?

"We should have given that guy a bunch of cress," Margaretta says. "Rats! I didn't think of it, he caught me off guard."

Up ahead, I see the culvert at Oyster Point Road. The car must be nearby. Nobody's after us. I am very cold, my bare feet are numb, I am fairly certain my face is bleeding.

"Hurry up," Margaretta says. "When we get in the car, I'll blast the heater. You'll be fine. Do you think this stuff will grow? I didn't see any springhouse back there. Was there one underground?" She doesn't wait for answers. "Up here. Come on. Think of the salads! Ruby lettuce, watercress. Watercress *salad*. My god! Elmer's in jail on principle, you know. He disobeys unjust laws, that's his job. I thought you used to have a dog. Didn't you have a dog?"

"Jean-Paul had a dog," I say.

"Yeah, that doesn't surprise me. Girl, what would it take to surprise me?"

IT IS LIKE the water, steaming, of a bath, her talk, the up and down stream of it, going over me, she doesn't expect anything in return. I can see the blue boxcar up on the shoulder of the road. Margaretta charges ahead. Her brown coat covers her to the ankles. She walks like a tree trunk walking, that color, that sway side to side, awkward, new at it, climbing the embankment.

AT A REST AREA on the turnpike, I clean up. I wash my face, duck my head in the shallow sink and wet my hair, wring it out until the water runs clear.

Margaretta wants to say hello, or good-bye, to Joseph Blue in Carlisle, and we pull off there, advance through the downtown, to the post office, and Lucy's apartment. My hair is still damp. Out of the car, my hair stiffens in the cold, it is almost freezing.

Margaretta knocks at the door of the apartment. She pushes the door – it is open – and we go inside. The place is deserted, not completely empty – I see the orange sofa. But no Lucy, no Aunt Charlaine Del Laraine.

"They've flown the coop," Margaretta says.

I THINK about Endorado, at the Super One store, of the times I go in there, and she isn't working, she isn't there. I want to ask somebody, "Is she missing?" But if they'd answer, as they would, "She's not here," it would be the same as saying, "Yes."

"Are they missing?" I ask Margaretta.

"Well, they're not here," she says. "They certainly aren't here."

I THINK I'll paint my fingernails purple. Like the hands of Endorado – mild, tainted. Writing, I could watch the motion of my own fingers, like synchronized winged things, insects, scarab-backed.

MARGARETTA walks through the rooms. She throws her coat over a folding chair, she looks in the cupboards.

"Okay," she says, "a lull. Kick off your shoes."

I've already done that, there they are, near the door. The mud on my feet has dried, it's that yellowish dust now, loesslike, a layer or two, on my legs.

IN FOUR PARTS

Sometimes, near the channel, air-hefted dust from the gravel, this color, settles on my shoulders, too, in my hair, and that's when Jack lifts me up, airy, and sets me down, I'm another layer of ground. What's the ground anywhere but thousands of years of everything's bone cells, bark cells, limb and skin, sinew, dried-down, blown about, settled.

"Dust makes me very happy," I say to Margaretta. I brush off my legs.

She fills a dishpan with warm water and sets it on the floor. "Here," she says, "soak your feet." And she picks up one foot, the whole of it like a child she'd help in a tub. And the other foot. With her hands like rags, she washes my feet, my ankles. The water goes gray, the silt washes down, you can understand how my feet disappear. Margaretta says, "There."

I believe if she'd wash my feet, and keep washing, until all the dirt was gone, I'd stand up, vacant below the knees. Empty air there.

Jack and I could kick up some winds.

MARGARETTA finds a stew pot in a cabinet and fills it with water, for her feet, too. On the sofa, she leans back, she shuts her eyes. She looks comfortable. See, even there, her feet crammed in a kettle.

I ASK Margaretta about the boxcars in Coatesville. Was there running water? How did they cook?

"I know," she says. "It's *always* a question of fire and water. Well, we breathed. We grilled fish, what do you think? Do you want to hear about blood, too? Murder? Illegitimate children?"

"I just want to hear you talk," I tell her.

"Well, then, I'll tell you about the cheese, and ice cream, the rowboat I found, and Venus rising."

"WHY DON'T YOU write," I say, "a sentence like that?"

Margaretta refuses to write. "I read," she says. "I'll *read* the sentence."

Her desire, she says, is to leave no trace. She is ruthless, petty in this.

She will write notes, sign checks, draw fish inside fish. These are scraps. And that suits her. The notes couldn't be put together and made into something whole. Nobody could track her, day to day.

She says, "When I'm done for, I want to be done."

Margaretta reads everything that Dorothea writes. She knows the pages won't last. What does it matter then?

I ask her.

Why *not* write it out – Coatesville, the handsaw on the nail?

Margaretta refuses. She says, no, she won't write anything. She'll talk. She'll tell everything. But, goddamn it, she will not *engrave* her words.

I TELL her I write what she says. I tell her, keep talking, your words won't be in stone. They'll *be* stone.

Who is endangered? The more in danger?

Margaretta laughs. She leans over, lopsided, on the sofa. Her hands fall together when she laughs, like the hands of Joseph Blue.

MARGARETTA picks things up. That's her education. She picks and chooses from the looks of things.

IN   FOUR   PARTS

She says, "I learned to read and write at the age of thirteen. Not be-fore. Before that, I couldn't spell out my own name."

Margaretta sits on the orange sofa, props her wet feet on the coffee table, and talks about a knife fight in the migrant camp at Coatesville. It begins at dusk.

"The sky across the west is streaked with lake-purple," Margaretta says. She says there is plenty of light, few shadows, and warm over-the-arm gusts of wind. This is July.

The fight begins in one of the boxcars. It does not concern a woman, no it is not that. This fight concerns a mozzarella cheese, shaped like a particular hill in West Virginia.

Margaretta draws the cheese in the air.

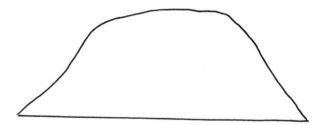

Two men, by chance, revere this hill.

These are the happenstance whys and hows of violence, Margaretta knows this.

One man, as a boy, had spent a summer on the hill in his grand-mother's cabin, and the other had hiked, the same year, down the east-ern slope of the hill with a girl cousin. Nothing else. They were boys then, unrelated, unknown to each other, before the age of summer work, or migrant up-and-down-the-coast work year-round.

The overall shape of this hill had, for years, consoled them, separately, as much as the memory of a lover's thighs, or the incline and the decline of a lover's back, buttocks.

THE HILL was, in fact, an ordinary hill, a mounded shape, wooded, with a few streams cut down the sides. That's all there was to it.

But decked out in summery green and calm – something completely unknown in the boxcar camp – the hill looms there, in their two minds.

The mozzarella cheese has to be cut to be eaten. The question is, how do you cut and divide and devour a hill?

BOTH MEN have knives. Everybody in the camp has knives – the children, boys and girls – to wing at trees, to slice, eat with, to cut stalks, leaves off cabbages, lettuces.

Margaretta, age ten, and her mother carry knives.

Margaretta wears a green-and-white checked dress this day, no buttons or snaps on it, but narrow strips of elastic at the waist, at the sleeves. The dress has a pocket of green canvas her mother has stitched on – for gum, for the knife. Margaretta swings her arms when she wears this dress. She's unencumbered, easygoing.

She cuts across the camp, hitting the edge of mud ruts, towards the fence at the edge of things, where she usually sits and watches Venus rising, slow, the sky purpling, blackening, top to bottom.

Nothing interrupts her or interferes with her stride.

Until the stumbling bodies of these two men, flung out-of-doors. They lurch in front of her. They roll, flail. No shirts on. They hit the mud, recover themselves, upright, on their knees.

The line of a cut bleeds, across the shoulder of one man. Margaretta is close enough to touch his skin.

She steps back, her hand in her pocket.

The man with the bleeding shoulder stands up. He wipes the muddy knife blade on his jeans to clean it, one side, the other side.

The other man hunkers down, breathes loud through his mouth – grunted breaths. He is larger, wide around the waist, tired. He stands up, loses his balance, and the two men fall together again, almost accidentally. They hold their knives well out to either side, while they push at each other with their free hands, and lean their heads, like boys, on each other's shoulders.

Margaretta watches the wrestling.

The bleeding man catches his right leg around the other man's left leg and pulls. The tired man buckles and falls back, tripped. He is rolling away even before he hits the ground. But the bleeding man is fast – he throws himself down, hits the other man with his full body weight, grabbing and holding the other man's arm, bent back at the elbow, in the dirt.

AT THE EDGE of the camp, early evening, no one is walking around. The fight is a thing to itself. Private. The boxcars, three rows of them, face the other way, their doors open that way, and windowless, the back walls are blank walls here. Wall next to wall. Margaretta looks around, deciding which way to go. She listens to the men, their loud, openmouthed suckings-in of air, the muffled collapses of one or the other, thrown down. They wrestle, one-armed, handicapped by the knives.

Venus is already bright. It will soon be dark. Margaretta's in no hurry.

MARGARETTA opens her left hand, now, years later. "Things took a turn," she says.

She shows the scar, a pale ridge. An extra line to read in her palm.

THE WOUNDED MAN, blood smeared on his chest, has had enough. It's getting dark. He stands back, grips the knife more securely.

The heavier man lunges to the side, throws himself to the side, as if he could pick himself up and toss himself clear. He takes two running steps, towards Margaretta. He grabs her by the arm. He pulls her around, in front of his chest, like a shield.

Margaretta is silent. She can feel the upheaval in the man's chest, his gasps, the weight of his fatigue. He is hardly able to stand. He leans on Margaretta and she buckles over at first. But he pulls her up, bends her back.

Margaretta smells the mud on his arms, the smell of horseflesh, or fish. The salt and muck smell of sweat, or cheese, or straw. These she will later think of, in lovemaking, as the smells of sex, of her own body's skin. But here, as a girl, she thinks only, I will stink.

THE MAN with blood on his chest comes at them, his hair matted with mud, the knife in his fist. One of his feet hits the mud, skids, slightly.

IN FOUR PARTS

Margaretta feels her arm pulled backwards. The man who holds her is in retreat. He frees her arm. But his hand grips her dress. He is dragging her backwards. She reaches into the green pocket of her dress, for the knife. The man, exhausted, will not let go of the dress. Has he forgotten she's inside it? He pulls her along. He tries to move fast. She loses her footing and stumbles. The man yanks at her. The green-and-white checked dress, with its elastic waist, pulls up, around Margaretta's neck.

The man yanks again. He cannot be looking.

The dress pulls up over her head, over her face. Margaretta shakes her arms, she is out of the dress.

Margaretta watches the man in retreat fall backwards, with this shift in balance. He is flat on his back.

Margaretta swings around. The wounded man with the knife is coming at her, swaying, like a drunken man. He staggers. He cannot be sure of his eyes, what he sees in front of him, there – a heavy, tired man replaced by a half-naked girl. Upright. Her narrow chest, the nipples small circles, her thin arms. The knife in her hand.

She stands still. She feels the air on her belly. Under her arms.

The bleeding man raises his knife, his arm is over her head. But she ducks, inside the bend of his body as he brings the knife down, and she pushes the blade of her knife into him, below his ribs. The soft tissues there.

She pushes upward, and she holds the handle of the knife until he falls, off to the side. It happens quietly, she hears nothing. The man's body settles against the ground, bent like a boy's in sleep, at the waist.

When Margaretta steps back, she hears cries from the man on the ground. She walks over to him, reaches a hand down to help him up. But his eyes are shut, he is howling, he swings his knife around, and it catches her, across the palm of her left hand.

Margaretta cries out. A short, low moan. Margaretta hears the wind hit the wall of the boxcar, invisible now, it is already dark.

MARGARETTA says it took a long time for her hand to heal. The palm of the hand opens and closes, even in sleep.

She doesn't say, in her telling of the fight, if the wounded man was dead, but of course he was. The other man, it's possible somebody helped him, buried the dead man by the fence the same night, it was not worth calling in the police. Margaretta had fallen asleep in the boxcar and didn't recognize, until years later, that a crime, or a number of crimes, had been committed.

The man who survived the fight said nothing to anybody about a young girl, undressed, with a knife, who was there, and then was not there.

MARGARETTA gets herself a glass of water. She's at home in the apartment. She sits on the sofa, pulls up her knees.

She tells me she cannot remember her first lover's name. She was so young, she remembers the food in the freezer instead. The white-paper-wrapped steaks. Half-gallon boxes of ice cream.

The man had a job in Philadelphia, she says. He stopped at a grocery store on his way home to buy ice cream for her. He cooked steaks, and they ate the ice cream – he sliced it like cake – in green glass bowls.

Margaretta cannot remember if the man kissed her. She thinks not.

THE KNIFE FIGHT. A lover. A child. The fish business.

By the time Margaretta could read, having done so much, she says she could handle whatever was in the books.

Or, was it, whatever was in the books, she laid claim to, took back. It was on a page, in her hands.

MARGARETTA read about Prague when she learned to read. A story about a schoolgirl in Prague, a river, and fishing. That's all Margaretta remembers. A clouded Pennsylvania sky over the old city. It was her favorite story.

The same year, in Coatesville, there was a spring flood. Fish swam across the fields, she says. She says her mother took her to a doctor. She says she had a child.

No details.

So I ask, "Was it a girl?"

"Sure, it's a girl."

Margaretta caught the fish stranded in ditches when the floodwater receded. She walked into the water and picked up the fish by hand.

With her knife, she cleaned them, set them out on a table. On ice from her lover's freezer.

He never knew she took the ice, sold the fish, gave up the child.

AFTER the flood, Margaretta finds a flat-bottomed rowboat across the road from camp. She drags it back for herself. The boat is small, light, shallow. A girl her size can pull it, or push off in it.

Early in the mornings, she hauls the boat across a field to a small farm pond and fishes. For a year, she skips work to fish.

The boat, like a shell, rocks with the water. Margaretta sits still, she uses a narrow board as an oar. The fish are so small, it is no strain to reel them in.

One day Margaretta takes off her shirt and lies down in the boat and sleeps. She dreams the city of Prague, in sunlight, its bridges polished, a fast current in the gray river, a rerouted river, out of Europe through the Mediterranean, a river across the Atlantic, a wrong-way current, warm, upstream into Brazil, upslope into the mountains. At the end were birds, fish the colors of birds, large snails on leaves.

Margaretta wakes in the boat to shouts. She sits up. She does not think to pull on her shirt. Air off the water rises, circles in her armpits.

A number of people stand on shore, a few kneel. Her mother lies on the ground.

Something has happened. Margaretta sees her mother's red shirt, the red shorts.

Slowly, Margaretta pulls the oar through the water and moves the boat closer. The air is cooler, each stroke.

On shore, they are rolling her mother over, onto her stomach, and pressing on her back.

Margaretta rows. Near to the shore, she sets the oar down.

Margaretta stands up. The boat shifts. Margaretta, with her arms, counterbalances. Then she stands there, arms at her sides, very still. She floats in.

Her mother's face is pressed sideways in the grass, her mother is empty, she looks flattened, emptied of whatever it was that shaped her face.

Margaretta, girl breasts aimed at her mother's eyes, rides the boat into the shallow water, until it scrapes shore.

I N F O U R P A R T S

HAD HER MOTHER seen the girl, safe in the small boat, she'd have lurched awake, shouted, Yes, there she is!

MARGARETTA talks until the room is dark. She would have preferred, she says, to have been completely naked, and her mother naked. She would have lifted her mother up and set her in the boat, and pushed off.

She believes she'd have fallen asleep again in the middle of the water. And in dream dived wih her mother into the gray river, where they'd have moved their arms with the current, under the bridges, they could have toured Prague, the wrong-way river, the Black Sea, Gibraltar, and on, trans-oceanic, to the high country of Brazil, lavish with canopied trees, green snakes, the edible flowering water plants, rooted all around.

MARGARETTA stretches out and sleeps for a while.

I take a shower, in a bathroom tiled in cobalt blue, a magnificent bathroom, with thick white towels and clean combs. Three toothbrushes, like stalks, stand in a white mug, hand-painted with large colorful birds.

We spend the night in the apartment. Nobody returns.

Margaretta is sure they're gone for good. She looks for Aunt Charlaine's purple robe, and can't find it. The refrigerator is empty except for a barbecued chicken, one, on a paper plate. The trash is collected in black plastic bags. The closets hold a few clothes, and empty hangers.

"They're gone," Margaretta says. "They're not coming back."

I drink some instant coffee and Margaretta ransacks the place. She takes slippers, bottles of spices – coriander, mustard seeds, cardamom, green peppercorns – a stainless steel Thermos bottle. She takes a black wool skirt and an orange windbreaker. When she's filled a couple of cardboard boxes, she quits. In large letters, she writes a note and props it on the sofa: STOPPED BY TO SAY HELLO. TOOK A THERMOS OF COFFEE. LOVE, MARGARETTA.

From here on out, Margaretta refers to The Winged Lucy, whenever she gets on the subject of Carlisle, a place of wonderment now. The episode with Joseph Blue becomes a great mystery for her, as indeed it is, since we lack any information or certifiable proof of anything any one of them claimed. There are dark rooms, the fabulous, well-lit bath, the questionable nature of family connection, Aunt Charlaine Del Laraine's threats, if that's what they were, the problematic course of Joseph Blue's life, The Winged Lucy and her studies in biological science, the appearances and disappearances of them all. All their talk. Margaretta's version of these. That's what there is. No papers on the premises, no identification, no books. No videotapes, no photographs. No drawings of pizza or fish.

THIS should not seem *too* strange, of course it's not, because, after all, after a night and a morning there, we're gone, too.

A RAIN settles in through the mountains of Pennsylvania, and low clouds cover everything around Pittsburgh. By the time we reach the Ohio border, the snow patches are washed from fields, and water lies on the flatlands, odd collections of it, mirrors, marking low spots.

I N F O U R P A R T S

I am rested, recouped. And so at the Cuyahoga, I ditch Margaretta, one last time. It comes as no surprise to her. We stop, she opens the door and says, "Okay. See you at the channel."

She stands there beside the Horizon, her brown coat unbuttoned – spring is evident, the first step, I can feel the ground has thawed.

We're in the ancient swamps, the residue of bygone lake beds, the thousand and thousand years of peat, muck on top of that, in some places, clay, sand, none of the water draining anywhere, but saturating, seeping back. Nothing flows aboveground, but underneath, fields hold a hidden pattern – with her coat hangers, Margaretta could chart the lines:

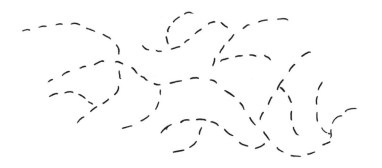

That's my map. The underground drainage tiles, dotted lines, a map of Midwest waterways, intricate, meshed. If the critical intersections were blocked, blasted, it would be easy to flood all of northern Ohio, Indiana, most of Michigan. Easy.

I DIG down. Immediately, I crack a tile. And what I am talking about now is a guerilla body, a physical shape I find hard to account for – like hand-thrown silt – pitched along through the pipes, the sections and in-tersections, mazes, against the onflow of water with terrific force until just ahead, just behind, the tiles crack or burst, a plume of mud, debris. On the surface, the sod arches, mole-tunnel traces, rivulets. Crisscrosses. At a factory foundation, or out in the middle of a field, wherever the tiles end, the silt body bears itself out, breaks the surface. What's left, look, is a giveaway trail – gray muck, gray water collecting.

Back and forth, through the ground between Cleveland and Kalama-zoo, the consequence of this tactic is the flood-letting of the lowlands, all of the ancient real estate of herons, muskrats, the breadth of the Black Swamp, a place where frogs, who knows when, burrowed deep to save themselves and only now with these explosions, fly out like shrapnel and rain down, their legs splayed.

YOU'VE SEEN it in the papers. The floodplains are flooded. Low-lands are lakes.

Given a body two-thirds water, the rest clay – and who isn't? – it's possible to do millions and then billions of dollars' worth of damage. Warmongers, movers and shakers, that's what they do. It is possible to disrupt whole populations, to operate like a force of nature.

And so – not-for-profit, undoing instead of doing, nobody the wiser – that's what I do, too.

FIRE

■ THE BODY

■　　　■　　　■　　　■　　　■　　　■　　　■

WHAT CAN I tell you about the morning, except that my hair, wet when I lay down, is dry now. Now it burns.

The floodplain is flooded. The channel is rising, filling its banks. It won't overflow. The city is built on a knoll, a knob.

What can I tell you about the morning, except that the flattened rolling cloud rising off the channel gets nowhere near Jean-Paul.

Jean-Paul rouses himself with Astral Weeks, or Bitches Brew – or then what? – Diamond Dogs.

But when he's awake and has thrown one dog-footed dance foot out of bed, he can tolerate anything on the airwaves, brand-new, S & L, Ground Zero, any of that, and by the time he's shaking his hair, the separate flames, he can even listen to reedy Avia Stendhal, echoey out in the middle of nothing. He blasts the voice, a wisp, into the corners of the room. He stands up, furious. He kicks one foot, shakes it, he kicks the other. He stretches his arms out, opens his palms, and the built-up charge, it is Sunday, with Sunday's full-blown political rage, the direct current from music to brain to spinal column, direct through his thighs, calves, and back again, thighs, testicles, penis, thighs, abdomen, penis, lungs – he breathes – the charge shakes his arms, exits with an amplified shocker twang, a slide off the dead-end rims of his fingernails.

He is electric. Not to be touched.

O U T S I D E, the cloud off the channel sizzles, at arm's length, or far-ther away, it condenses, and a pathway opens, cleared of fog, warmed up, an atmospheric architecture that accompanies Jean-Paul's maneu-vers. He spins his arms, the currents cut away through mists. He's an engine. A fan. Never far from music, noise, whether making it or trans-mitting it, grrraahhnng, crreeeeiii. Kkhhsssst.

He charms animals, he is proud of that, not with melodic tunes but with insect rackets, calls, yodeled and snarled, whistled lures, the daily incomprehensible coos, hisses, that loosen the tautness of any fleshed body, mammal or no.

It's a creaturely world, becalmed, bemused, revealed where it lies, pauses. Somehow Jean-Paul illuminates hideouts. Nests, lairs, the eyes of all things that have eyes, that's what it's possible to see.

Animals turn at the approach of his fiery head, their eyes shine. And what you've got is a populous place, wherever he goes, alleyways, woods, many pairs of eyes, many more than you'd guess.

It's why I don't mind the disruption, the early morning, dark over-head, when Jean-Paul opens the door, exits. We're out.

Even in the open, vibrations from the stereo shake through his hair, he carries residues of sound, wound with the flame curls, he is animated, nervy.

He heads through town, watching side to side, and first, down an alley, first thing, there are the pairs of eyes, yellow discs, or silvery, tin-seled circles – low between trash bins, on the branches of sumac stunted in concrete, on platforms of fire escapes. Rats, raccoons, opossum, dogs, cats, insects, bats, it's too dark to see the bodies, but the animals, wherever they are, whatever they are, Jean-Paul can't tell, they turn, they blink.

In the middle of the city, Jean-Paul takes a right, exits the downtown office plazas, blocks of hotels, wall-to-wall. It is still dark, there are eyes below the grates in the sidewalk, eyes in the cornices, suspended, two dozen stories up, ledges busy with eyes. And as people appear out-of-doors, at the newsstand, their eyes are visible, too, large, variable eyes.

JEAN-PAUL sees as many signs of life as a man can see. He ignores a good many things, though, too. That's plain. He ignores water, and plant life, fuel lines, brick walls.

He could detonate anything flammable – trash, chemicals, natural gas, kerosene storage tanks, refineries, munitions factories, forests – but he hasn't bent his head, even to light a match. He's no threat. The fire's contained.

S. does the dirty work. Jean-Paul fumes.

Jean-Paul kicks. He's a man torn away, cut loose, you could say, cut out of his culture. If it weren't for electronic sound effects – decibeled, woofered and tweetered – he'd be disconnected entirely, left to his own resources, and another continent's clothes.

YOU CAN SEE that his hair's on fire, but what else can you see?

Is he a man?

You ask the question. You point.

A good question. How can he be, as he is, housed in a body with girl breasts and woman-hard heart. Jean-Paul claims, *c'est facile*. That is very easy, mine is the body you dare not interrogate, dare not, without invitation, touch, and what you don't touch, sweetheart, you don't know anything about. And anyway, Jean-Paul insists, when I wish, in private, I appear. Our brother Jack, recall, is invisible, entirely, he's nothing but air, how do you snag him?

JEAN-PAUL does not need to prove himself, that's what his thinking is, apparently. There is no self-doubt. He accommodates, waits his turn, his time. Dorothea washes over, sodden as she is, but sooner or later, Jean-Paul wakes, he insinuates, he snares, he charges up the mind, and you can see it happening, first, in the eyes, and then, it is like hot water, the steam, banging in pipes, the blood surges, he transfuses the whole system, the hair ignites, and there he is, shoulders a bit rounded, hair in copper coils on his chest, penis, balls, secure in his tight pants, who dares pull at him, ask, are you really a man, ask, prove it, who dares?

I do, of course. It pleases me, the blatant terms, the contradictions, the disputable matters of who's who. The irrefutable claims of words over all else. I listen to what he says.

Jean-Paul speaks French, his native tongue, and English does not work for him as it does for you and me. If he says, for instance, "And anyway, when I wish, in private, I appear," you must wonder about the phrases, any of them, the compromises he may have made with the language. If the words were "*quand on veut . . . j'arrive*," for instance, the whole thing is problematic, referents and subjects much less clear than English would let you think.

NOT MANY BLOCKS from downtown, via the alley route, the pavement slopes. A smell of sludge and oil, mud and fish, rises, and then the channel is visible, a gray belt of water.

Jean-Paul coughs. He shakes his head, he riles his hair.

In the 24-hour parking lot, he sits on a wooden step at the channel brink. The banks slope down steeply, weeded, both sides lie in darkness. Jean-Paul whistles. A rasping, percussive whistle, he is thinking of noise-maker sounds he heard, where was it, those Brazilians?

Jean-Paul turns his head slowly. He whistles again.

ACROSS THE CHANNEL, in the flat black scrub and grasses, where there'd been nothing to see, look, you can see where the animals are.

Small lights glow in the reeds at the water's edge, and upslope, in the underbrush.

Foxes curl, half-twists in dens, eyes not quite round. Under grasses, leaves, shelters for mice, dozens of star-point eyes cluster – it is like the night sky. All along the banks of the channel, innumerable hooded ani-mal lights, dark spaces between.

THESE WALKS before dawn, this is the company I desire. The rest of the time with Jean-Paul, he is too showy, that lion stalk he has. His growls. Dancing, yes, we do that, some nights. Maybe it's the daylight, the sun itself, that irks, no, more likely, excites him. His arrival in the house signals a crisis, some quarrel I've got with S., for instance, Jean-

Paul there, on principle, to take her side. He speaks for her, rages, stamps his heels on the floor. He turns on the radio, hits the volume. Outside, he is milder, that's true. Tamed. In the midst of animals, I suppose, he settles down, he knows they're there, he crosses their trails, catches their scent, appreciates their secrecy. When he steps on the droppings of a fox, when he notices an owl's regurgitated pellets, he closes his lips, hushed.

The nights Jean-Paul sleeps under a roof, he sleeps like a beast, curled up. He breathes. He smells sour.

That's how I know he's there.

IN THE EARLIEST weak light, Margaretta is out and about. She sets up her fish stand near the pier, and Jean-Paul walks over. He helps her unlatch the fold-down countertop, he arranges the waxed paper, the knives, for her.

"What I like about you, Jean-Paul," Margaretta says, "is that noise you make in the back of your nose."

Jean-Paul grunts, it sounds like *on* in French, the back of the throat nasality. *On, on.*

Margaretta says, "Have some coffee. Sit down."

She hands him a damp assortment of Dorothea's pages. They sit on the pier in the gray light.

Jean-Paul leafs through the papers, a few pages. His hair blows in the wind, warms the air between them.

"So you had a dog at one time?" Margaretta says.

"A setter."

"I think I remember seeing that dog." Margaretta tosses a chunk of

hale-dust with her heels
ntil she could press her toes
bone.

Absolutely," she said.

Jonasine said it wouldn't be
sy, putting together cameras,
e sets, there would be in-
dible technical problems,
en the location.

Whatever we need, we'll
vent," Andalusia said.

t was, in fact, Andalusia's
ity to fabricate – just about
thing, out of materials at hand—
t landed her all of the parts,
d most of the credits, rolling
at the end, line after line.

S?" Margaretta says.

nds settled," Jean-Paul says "She's got what she wants, that's
s like to me. When you plant the watercress, you watch,"
"she probably won't lift pen to paper again."

gravel into the channel. "The one that sat down when you said Fetch."

"Fetch was its name, that's the one. I learned how to walk, walking that dog." Jean-Paul presses Dorothea's papers, he flattens them out on his knees.

"Go ahead," Margaretta says. "Read your waterlogged sister," she says. "Let's hear it."

Andalusia Gets the Part
— by S. Campbell

It was a lull, an air pocket over the ocean, that brought Andalusia down. Sure enough, she was swallowed up.

Jonasine said, "Have a seat."

On the belly of the whale, Andalusia made herself at home.

They shared a snack and Andalusia described how she'd circumscribed the globe, in a balloon she'd designed herself. She explained how she redecorated her balloon, place to place, various camouflages — she redid its painting to desert, when

there was desert and she was
flying low; to mottled clouds
over landmasses; to thin strips
of white, airbrushed to almost
nothing for sea crossings. Or
else she painted blatant images
nobody could miss: the streamy-
hair heads of women, a collage
of huge eyes, or the uprooted
tree design.

Andalusia made her flights a
display, not for marketing, she
said, and not to break records —
she never checked into any of
that. She liked the liftoff. The
suspension. When she needed a
break, she set the balloon down,
wherever, and got a job as a
mechanic, or actor, or junkwoman,
until she could muster money,
or enough local support, to repaint
and move on.

Andalusia asked, "What's to do
here?"

Looking around,
debris, the Dumpst
of the whale. For
Jonasine talked
expert talk.

Andalusia took
sine's boxes of
work, her reject
through the eve
talked cinema.
she had worked
and Canada. She
difficulty of fil
the tundra — a
with a city bui
production, she
one black, one

Her mimicry
was precise,
convincing as

"Can you h
two?" Jonasi

Andalusia
dals and d

"NO GUN
"She sou
what it sound
Jean-Paul says

THE SKY ALTERS, almost mechanically, from gray to twists of pink in the East.

Margaretta asks if Jean-Paul would like to drive with her to Morenci. To make inquiries.

She wants to see if Joseph Blue hitched a ride back, walked, whatever, from Pennsylvania. If he brought back The Winged Lucy and Aunt Charlaine.

"Some people you've got to keep track of," she says, "even if they're strangers. There's no other point to talk—you find out who you want to keep track of, and who you don't."

"Who *don't* you?" Jean-Paul asks.

Margaretta pours out two more cups of coffee, she stares at Jean-Paul's hair. "Well," she says, "You don't have to bother with people who know what they're doing. They go along, that's it. There's no reason to keep track of them."

"Who keeps track of you?"

Margaretta pushes her finger at him. "Look who's here. Just look who's here."

"I happen to be in the vicinity," Jean-Paul says.

"And so are a hundred thousand other people. But, look, you're here. A few people stay in touch, long-distance. Elmer does. Some stop by. I've got friends. But this Joseph Blue, I just thought we could drive down there, how about it, and see what's going on."

MARGARETTA drives. We follow the roads she's highlighted on the map, an easy drive, right-angle roads on flat land. Jean-Paul, nervous and unruly, navigates.

IN FOUR PARTS

"What if he's not home?" Jean-Paul says.

"It doesn't matter if he's not home," Margaretta says. "I just want to take a look."

"About an inch to go," Jean-Paul says. He presses his thumb on the map.

"Blue is so tenderhearted," Margaretta says, "he won't drive over 55. He's never hit anything."

"Me neither," Jean-Paul says.

"I've hit a couple of cats," Margaretta says. "It's no fun."

A mile outside the Morenci city limits, at a mailbox with the name Joseph Blue hand-painted in cursive, we turn onto a gravel driveway.

The gravel is thick, dishpan deep. Margaretta hits the brakes.

The car sinks in, keels to one side. Jean-Paul lurches – his head knocks the windshield – and his hair, in long forward-falling strips, flies up against the glass.

But after that, it's a lullaby ride, cushy, with time for us to blink and look out one window, and then turn and look out the other. Those two minutes, maybe three minutes, driving the gravel road to Joseph Blue's front door, add up to the real trip. The rest is just *en route*.

SOME RIDES, across open landscapes, on the turnpikes, suggest the layout of the whole planet. The horizon scrolls away, and you're aware that the road is a line, as visible as the Amazon, on a satellite photograph. Other rides, especially under the cover of trees, whether it's winter or summer, are more secret. You might as well drive under a tent, or camouflaged netting. What you see is something close up, as if you were looking into a diorama, one scene, the furnished mind, say, of a particular climate, or soil. Rocks, moss, birdfoot trefoil. Unless a human being has been at work. And then, of course, what you see are the furnishings of a brain, lifted from the imagination and set out there – they might as well be sofas – among the trees.

This is a camouflage drive, and here, between the trunks of trees, stand – I will say it plain: white-painted rocks – one rock on top of another rock, mortared together.

I guess they are mortared together. Or concreted.

Not sofas. But they might as well be sofas.

An arrangement of the two-part rocks, solid, unadorned, is grouped beside a wire fence. Several others, here and there, have been sprayed with green glitter, a few swipes of it, so that finally Jean-Paul says, "What the hell!"

Margaretta says, "Look around!"

There are tires, in heaps – that's not so unusual off these side roads, and stacks of split wood. But also, there is a pine tree decorated with plastic gallon milk jugs, strings of them. Under the tree, three wheelbarrows. A six-foot heap of leaves. Farther on, a shed fallen in, the roof flat on the ground, with an antique paneled door propped in front, a white porcelain doorknob. A burned-out Volkswagen. Straw bales set up, with a bow target. Iron wheels.

Margaretta says, "God, it's a mixed economy out there."

Off by itself, sinking into the ground, there is somebody's rusted grain drill, horse hitch intact. On the low branches of trees, bird feeders of all sorts – tube feeders, flat plate feeders, red plastic alpine house feeders, hummingbird feeders.

"I don't know what to think," Margaretta says.

OF COURSE I'd heard Joseph Blue's talk and Margaretta's account of Carlisle – but words in the air, what are they? Words in the air! Suspended things, like stars – they suspend time, too, they confuse its terms. Stars hang about in space, we see them, but they're outdated, old when the light reaches us, some of them already long gone – we don't know which ones – already darkened, exploded.

THIS ISN'T hearsay, though.

Here is Joseph Blue's driveway, his stonework constructions, the thin woodlot with objects among the trees, and his frame house up ahead, at the last turn.

Joseph Blue could appear at the door, in this place, and he wouldn't have to say, "I'm Joseph Blue. I've lived these and these different lives – because I say so. I've worked these jobs. Here I am." He wouldn't have to say anything in particular. That is, it wouldn't matter what he said here, it would match the surroundings, one way or another, there is such a conglomeration of things, not just *anything*, but these things, placed by hand.

Apparently he isn't a person to hide his trash or calculate effects. Anybody can see, he isn't out to please.

"CHARLAINE'S a security guard," Margaretta says to Jean-Paul. "White hair, a registered pistol – no, I don't know if it's registered. Lucy's a young naturalist. I saw her report on spotted salamanders."

"Don't you ever run into regular wage earners?" Jean-Paul says.

"Charlaine earns wages. It's a regular job," Margaretta says.

"You know what I mean. You could once in a while pay attention to people with something going for them. Incomes. You could drive up their driveways. There've got to be a couple of interesting rich people someplace."

"Lucy's in school. That's employment," Margaretta says. "Anyway, what do you do?"

Jean-Paul smiles.

"Oh?" Margaretta says.

Jean-Paul shakes his hair, stretches out his feet in black Rive Gauche boots, and says, "Okay, why don't you come along dancing with us tonight? Invite your friend Joseph here, and Charlaine."

"I don't know if they're here. I thought maybe he brought them along back. We'll see."

MARGARETTA stops the car near the house.

The paint is bad in a few places, peeled to gray boards, but the windows are all in one piece, glazed, the frames carefully painted.

We step out onto ground heaved from the thaw, brown and crusted with winter debris – the flattened leaves with a press of mold on them, pine needles stuck at odd angles in the dirt. The air smells sweet – molasses, a sorghum and silage smell. I can't trace it. Gum, or pitch.

AT THE EDGE of the driveway, I push at a log with my foot, roll it over. It's spongy with rot, jammed with termites, an incredible roiling clump of them where the wood has touched ground. One termite sticks to my boot – there isn't much to it – a couple of soft see-through cells.

MARGARETTA knocks at the front door and calls out, "Blue!"

Jean-Paul, beside the car, takes two steps into a triangle of sunlight. He slings his head back and shuts his eyes, basking as few can bask in March, when it's leafless, and the wind cuts. His hair lifts, curls, and it worries me – no, it doesn't worry me, I suppose it surprises me – seeing him here in the open air, in daylight, the fire on his head less vivid, calmed, no animals in sight.

Margaretta knocks again.

I don't mind the waiting around. I stomp my feet. Wherever I hit the ground, it breathes out, that unmistakable exhale, collapse, of early spring.

ENDORADO, at Super One, stamps her right foot, too, I've seen it, for emphasis when she talks. Her cushioned all-purpose shoe compresses, something like a lung, when it hits the tile of the floor. If you listen in a store, along with the music, there's all of the ordinary air in and out, from shoes, from mouths.

I WALK in a circle, out towards a propane tank, back by the edge of some swampy ground, the water still frozen, with a hard-candy brittle surface, easy to crack. Tap with a toe, it cracks.

"Blue! Are you home?" Margaretta walks to a side door, opens the aluminum storm door and knocks hard. "Blue!"

If Lucy Del Laraine has interest in the comings and goings of the natural world, she could conduct some detailed studies here. Aunt Charlaine could guard the grounds – they could claim the place as an off-road refuge! A sign could read: This Is Not a Subdivison.

MARGARETTA waves to Jean-Paul, come here, and he turns towards the house.

In the steps I take from the trees to the yard, I pass three wooden crates level-full with gravel, ten green glass bottles in a circle, a trough full of cracked corn, a tree box for wood ducks, a handsaw on top of a red toolbox, dozens of black plastic planters, empty, or upside down, bricks arranged around a hole – a fire pit? – a compost heap with weeds on top, bronzed from freeze; two whole cucumbers on a rock; nails, hinges, six or seven toy tractors, dump trucks, collected at the base of a tree.

Nothing is prettified, nothing is cleaned up to cover the orders of decay, the only orders in the long run, no matter how many designers or cleaning crews a person pays.

Joseph Blue has paid nothing to anybody, that's for sure. Would Aunt Charlaine – you have to wonder – approaching the house, have closed her eyes, regretted the move? Would Lucy, her heart speeding up, have pulled out pen and paper, and said, "I don't know where to start – there's so much."

I WALK past a shirt, lake-purple, and a towel-shaped fabric, hung on a clothesline tied to two trees. I see more birds than I've seen in one place in years – blue jays, cardinals, black-capped chickadees, dozens of house finches, nuthatches, woodpeckers, mourning doves, gold finches, four pheasants, two quail, crows in the trees, juncos on the ground. At one of the windows of the house, I see a hand – it's a small birdlike hand – wave.

AT THE WALK to the house, Jean-Paul shakes his head. His hair sways side to side, very slow.

Margaretta steps away from the door. "He doesn't have a plan," she says. "He likes to do one thing, and then he likes to do something else. That's all. He doesn't read the right books."

Margaretta isn't apologizing for Joseph Blue. "These are the god-damn facts," she says.

BY THE TIME Joseph Blue with his two-part hair appears on the porch and embraces Margaretta and lifts her up until her feet clear the ground, by the time he looks at Jean-Paul and says "Your hair is on fire, man!" it's no longer a question of why Margaretta has tracked him down.

Jean-Paul shakes his head.

But it doesn't surprise me that Aunt Charlaine probably said "Sure, let's go" and left the rented apartment and comfortable bath, and that Lucy Del Laraine, with her girlhood love for the multiplicity of things, sits inside the house, at this moment, sketching termites, or beetles, or an oddball arrangement of papershell freshwater clams, from life.

IT'S A SHORT afternoon, a few words. Jean-Paul sits in the dark living room and taps his foot. He watches Lucy, at her desk. He watches the feet of Aunt Charlaine, asleep in the next room on a bed, her feet in oversize tube socks, maybe Joseph Blue's. Her toes point out, northeast and northwest.

IN THE KITCHEN, Joseph Blue asks Margaretta, "On the road, have you ever met up with a dangerous man?"

"Not for long," she says. "I can tell right away."

"What if you're wrong?" Joseph Blue says.

"I'm wrong about many things, but I'm always right about that. Violence smells fishy."

"You smell fishy!" Joseph Blue says.

"Violence smells fishy on men, I mean," Margaretta says. "You smell like soup, Joseph Blue. You don't worry me."

MARGARETTA gives Joseph Blue her address and tells him to send The Winged Lucy's writings, or stop by, and so on and so on, she kisses him on the neck. She admires Lucy's drawings, she takes plenty of time, she waves to the sleeping Aunt Charlaine on the way out.

I am an admirer of Margaretta's exits. She never wants to leave where she is, but she also wants to be off to another place, attending to something else. There's a reluctance in her to say good-bye, then, and she drags it out. But she's headed towards the door, and when she's through it, that's it, her mind turns to the next thing.

IN   FOUR   PARTS

IT MUST be a talent, like a swimmer's steady strokes, and the turn of the head in water for each gulp of air. Endorado makes these turns, too, from the crushing machine to a customer, from a customer to her checkout friend, but how can it be so simple? Keeping one thing to one side, and another to another? Confusion here, calm here. Shelley and Mike, Endorado and friend. Fire, water. Indoors, outdoors. Or, more simply, she, he. One, the other. How does a person keep an even keel?

JEAN-PAUL stands at the car, kicking the front tire.

Margaretta says. "Let's plant the watercress. How's that?"

"Dorothea can sharpen her knives," Jean-Paul says. "The salad's on its way. You've done a good deed."

They are ganging up, in their generous and for-the-minute non-violent natures.

And I think, all right. I admit it. I have never done a good deed, on the one hand, without, on the other, blasting something to smithereens.

BACK AT THE channel, Margaretta opens the hatch of the Horizon. We walk across the gravel, hauling buckets, to the edge of the water. We sit for a while. Margaretta hums.

Jean-Paul tries to match the sound of the buses, accelerating, the engine sounds, the tires on pavement. He hums certain chords, by vibrating the cartilage in his nose. He makes sounds like kazoos. Like buses, accelerating.

MARGARETTA'S hair is streaked and spiked today. Gray, platinum, blond, burgundy, chestnut, blue. It doesn't look extravagant. No. I tell her she looks like a woman with a lot on her mind.

"That's me," she says.

A woman who could get in her car and drive in any direction.

"That's it. Aimless. It's how I can stay in one place," she says, "and be far-flung."

THE SKY has clouded, dark and light kneaded twists, the rolls of a frontal system, Arctic air coming in.

Jean-Paul takes an armload of plants.

The water in the channel is churned up, cold, but Jean-Paul doesn't care, he walks right in.

He follows the bank to a shallow cove, a leggy spit of clay. Margaretta says, "Good." And Jean-Paul pushes the roots down, anchors a few in mud to get them started. If they take, the plants will web themselves shore to shore, they won't need dirt.

Margaretta lifts out more plants, she hands them along.

Jean-Paul pushes his hands down deeper. He rolls up his sleeves. Water overflows his boots.

The plants spread out, an S-curve, white-leaved, like nothing else.

We step back and consider, like gardeners, will the plants wilt, or grow green? Does it make sense to trim them back, or not? We watch the leaves shift, ghostly, in the current. Margaretta says, "Leave them alone."

IN   FOUR   PARTS

DOROTHEA has not made a move. Jean-Paul pulls off his boots. "I'll tell her," he says.

"Go ahead," Margaretta says. "See what she thinks. Catch me some fish. Bring me something she's written. Watch out for knives. Don't get pneumonia!"

JEAN-PAUL has never got pneumonia. He coughs. But he never gets sick, he never has a fever, he does not cut himself, he does not burn.

JEAN-PAUL takes off his shirt. He walks in.

There's no mystery to it. Underwater, his hair cannot be extinguished. When he drops in on Dorothea, the flames don't hiss, they don't fizzle. In fact, they flare, an oxygenated burst, in the first whoosh underwater, Jean-Paul dives and his hair streams out behind him, his hair glows, rich in orange and purpled shadings, coal and ember and intense yellow tips—he's phenomenal there, fire and water puzzled together—the pieces fit, a line no more than a razor cut, a fluid line, between the strip that is flame and the strip that is water.

IT'S A livable place, in a way.

Jean-Paul settles himself across the table from S. His hair flows over his shoulders, like hers, in wide strands, nothing outlandish, supsended in the water, slow, variable in direction.

He says, "It is safer to kiss you here. What can ignite?"

S. leans across the table and kisses him on the mouth.

Their hair confuses the issue, it's an astounding thing to see, it's one of those molten flows, eruptive, honey and salmon braids. When you see the amalgamation of water and fire – you know it. The elements defy their own laws. On seaside volcanic slopes you see it – rock and fire assuming the laws of water, flowing together, lava rolls like the ocean breakers swelling, raised, crested, frilled, keeled over, wound around, spumed, sprawled.

THEY ARE underwater. They sit at the table and the woman – she is a woman, with breasts washed by currents, with hair floating like open fans over her – says a few phrases. Whatever it is she says, the man opposite her – and he is a man: his penis floats at ease in his lap – reacts with an expression of surprise. His mouth opens, water flows there, the jaw drops farther, and his eyes shut.

When language is indistinguishable from water and water is indistinguishable from air, the common denominators are plain.

Their talk resembles breathing, and words in themselves matter less than the out and in, the exchange.

They exchange, it could be said, what is tolerable for what is not. The exact mechanism is impossible to determine: whether, for instance, the tolerable is spoken and the intolerable heard and incorporated. Or the other way around.

IT IS THE dream of the body – to know a place bodily and to say so. To take words into and out of itself. To have words assume bodily shape,

IN FOUR PARTS

salamander or *milk*, it doesn't matter. To inhabit a shore, a fabulous body of water, debris, insects drilled in the sand.

Where in the world can the body say, I am in my element?

The body strips to its flesh, and flame, and dives. When air gives out, and blues and greens simplify into dark, lips open the way lips open for kisses.

But the body, more fully desirous, recalcitrant in the extreme, says, even there, No, this is not the world I dreamed of. This is not the world.

A I R

■ T H E B O D Y

∎   ∎   ∎   ∎   ∎   ∎   ∎

IT'S DARK. The floodplain is flooded.

In the lowlands, in the low-lying wheat fields, across the paved, unlit malls, water rises and keeps rising. It inches up the posts of street signs.

It darkens the trunks of trees, a push of water when the wind hits, and then the gradual overtaking of the lowest limbs. Roads run into lakes now and cars turn back. People pack up belongings from cottages, from glass-walled rooms on the river, and haul them, day and night, upslope.

There is no panic. This happens slowly, as the ground thaws. As it rains. It happens slowly, the way arctic melt will happen, with time for despair. There is despair.

But then again, it is more than that. Despair for the shoes, the fireplaces and walls, the gardens gone. But also, astonishment – with the unforeseen change of scene. People ooh and ahhh. They notice the lay of the land. They sit down on hillsides and watch the water. In cities, they camp out on high ground.

This evening, Margaretta says to the last customer, "The water smells different. There's more of a ground smell to it."

They sniff the air.

I am picking up cans left on the pier. I have five cans in a sack. Fifty cents.

Margaretta waves her arms. "Hang in there!" she shouts. "Vote!"

"Run for governor!" I shout back. I mean it. Who else will tax the rich? Get a few things done. Well, look around. Who? Who else embrace the anomalous? Egg it on. Denounce injustice? Salvage wetlands. Pay a visit to Joseph Blue. Haul me around. Witch water. Carry a knife. Loll about with the contradictions, the convolutions of any populace.

Except for her hair, Margaretta hasn't been groomed. She'd get my vote.

"I'll write in your name," I tell her.

"Good," she says. "Me, too. I'll write that much. How many votes do we add up to?"

MARGARETTA takes the combs out of her hair. She bends over, shakes her head. The light at the fish stand is on, I watch her blunt shadow, the blurred disturbances of her hair.

She walks towards the channel, she stretches her arms, pushing them forward, up over her head. She walks away, then stops, and I know she has reached the place where we planted the watercress.

Margaretta sits on a bench at the water. She takes off one shoe. She slips off her knee-high stocking. With both hands, she rubs her foot. She rubs her big toe. Then, she bends, bends farther, and sticks the big toe in her mouth. Why? Does it hurt? Her big toe in her mouth. She sucks her big toe.

She's folded herself up like a sea thing, there on the bench.

But in a minute, Margaretta sits back. She exercises her knees. She takes off her other shoe. And, shoes in hand, she gets up, walks off to the edge of the water, one foot stockinged, one foot bare – but both feet are damp, they have to be, pressed into dirt, on the gravel, on the concrete there, on broken glass, in patches of oil-washed water, in air, momentarily, one foot then the other, sullied, that's her, she doesn't bypass the matted-up papers, or sequins, or crabgrass, or spit.

I know what she's seeing: nothing that looks real. Dark ground, dark water, dark sky. White leaves, floating.

What I see looks real enough: Margaretta on her way home. In the dark. Margaretta who drives East. Who is all talk. All torso and arms and legs. Who is not in front of anything and not behind anything. Who reads until she falls asleep. Who sleeps well.

As for me, I do not sleep well.

THE FLOODPLAIN is flooded, dry ground is dry.

Margaretta says fishing is good.

I sleep, and wake, feverish, chilled.

Jack is in the air.

With Jack, I am always myself. The door opens. Losses, invisibilities, collect like real things, not far out of reach – four apples turned to knuckle on the tree in March, starved limbs; the rice-paper shells of flies, on the floor for weeks; chestnuts, smooth in the bowl as skulls, the tenderness to the hand when you stir and stir through them.

The air fills up with griefs, global, they are fully themselves, not abstract, not generalized out of their shapes, not blurred.

Jack is a juggler – he tosses these things, one after another – and he's a magician, too – they stay in the air, suspended. The weightlessness of his approach, the way he kisses me on the lips, it is barely a touch at first, but then his tongue traces the rim of the lip, outlines it, this is the mouth.

Yes, it is. Remember. He kisses one lip, the other. He does not say where he has been, gathering up all these presents.

He offers me so much to mourn, it is his generosity, it does not make me sad. What else could he bring me worth more?

He is the one, when a man or a woman's body is soaked with sweat, rigid, awake, who takes the clotted air from the room, washes it out, cleans up, and says the word, sleep.

That's the laundry he carries in heaps when he walks in here. Scarecrow. Junkman. Hobo. Scrounger. The coast-to-coast three a.m. flotsam, sweet, bloody, arrives with him, arms in the air, there's the noise of wings, cloth, cutting loose, hovering. He shakes out the papery flies from the sheets, the hairs from the bedclothes.

Jack is the one I love most, he's afraid of nothing.

There's not much to him, and that way, there's not much to lose. He never quits.

I turn on the heater, dust snaps in the coils, the air lifts, balloons, Jack touches my hands now, my thighs. He takes off my clothes, they drift over that way. He says, "What if I trim your hair?"

He points to the ragged cuts behind my ear, he pulls the hair upward, there's a scent of marsh grass, sourweed. He combs my hair with his fingers, the chopped unevenness of it leads one hand before the other, and the air and its swampland remnants, all around, pulse, with the waves he makes, hand over hand. It is a wonderful thing for the skin, clayey, unscrubbed, to be indoors among marsh smells or weeds. In the same way it is a wonderful thing for the skin to be outdoors, aired, among books, kettles, or floors. The more of this mix, this confusion, and with Jack it is all confusion, the more I can move about, and speak for myself. With Jack, I say "Yes." I say "Cut." I don't think I've ever said "No," not with him.

I know where I am. I am down the street from Margaretta, upstairs in a room with two doors, two windows.

Jack turns on the radio. He combs my hair. He trims it, straight at the shoulders, I feel the blade. The orchestra on the radio begins the fourth act, *André Chénier*, there's not much hope at that point, any audience knows it, but what are the violins supposed to do, lie down in the laps of musicians, refuse to go on? There's a woman now, too, in the jail – hear her? – the precision of her phrases, what's she saying?, nobody believes her although she's got it by heart – not a stutter, like a halo she's figured out how to exchange, a send-off – those poets! – words, they have figured it out, are the surest way to the guillotine.

Jack says, "That's better."

I look in the mirror. My hair is damp. It's a good cut.

"On the way over here," Jack says, "I heard geese coming down in the dark."

We go downstairs and out the back door. One step. The grass is there, but it's heavy with dew, the first step outside is a step into water.

There are no lights along the channel here, no lights in the house. In the darkness that feels like layers of air, fabrics, I can't see my feet. But I turn my head. We listen.

We hear the geese. Somewhere out there, in the channel, they're honking. A few, then more. Then the muffled sounds of wings. Calls overhead, much closer, and closer, how do they navigate in the dark?, a flock coming in from a field, approaching the water, gliding down.

There's the rush of air through wings, there's no way to guess how many are landing, the water splashes, washes, in waves. There is nothing to see.

We wait. It's quiet. We listen, and it is the same as watching. We know the geese are swimming, some with their necks raised, stretched, some preening, some with their heads ably twisted back on the body, asleep, webbed feet under the water, stirring whatever's there, Dorothea, Jean-Paul's hair, waterweeds, the geese are not drifting, they are breathing invisible air. Jack's air.

In the dark Jack assumes the spaces between the bodies of things, he fills in the blanks. In the dark, he is every shape, as a matter of fact, and the geese in the dark, after Jack has said his farewells, close their eyes and sleep on the water, and circle, and wake, and sleep again, and not one collides with another, there is no room there, or anywhere, for that to happen.

Janet Kauffman has written two collections of short fiction, *Places in the World a Woman Could Walk* and *Obscene Gestures for Women*, as well as the novel *Collaborators* and two books of poetry, *The Weather Book* and *Where the World Is*. She lives in Michigan.

This book was designed by Tree Swenson.

It is set in Joanna type

by The Typeworks with handwriting by Anne Czarniecki and

manufactured by Maple – Vail

on acid-free paper.